By Aidan Wayne

Hitting the Mark

Published by Harmony Ink Press
Showers, Flowers, and Fangs

Published by Dreamspinner Press
www.dreamspinnerpress.com

HITTING THE MARK

AIDAN WAYNE

Published by
DREAMSPINNER PRESS

5032 Capital Circle SW, Suite 2, PMB# 279, Tallahassee, FL 32305-7886 USA
www.dreamspinnerpress.com

Trade Paperback ISBN: 978-1-64405-149-8
Digital ISBN: 978-1-64405-143-6
Library of Congress Control Number: 2018963157
Trade Paperback published May 2019
v. 1.0

Printed in the United States of America
♾
This paper meets the requirements of
ANSI/NISO Z39.48-1992 (Permanence of Paper).

Chapter One

MARCUS COULDN'T remember the last time he was this nervous.

Well, okay, maybe he could. His first audition all those years ago, the one that had gotten him a speaking role on a feature film…. He'd about shaken out of his sneakers before stepping in front of that camera.

He'd come a long way since then. Now he was known for action-packed movies with passion-powered romances, famous for doing his own stunts and fight scenes. He'd been on six different World's Most Eligible Bachelors lists in the last year alone, renowned for not only his acting but his physical skill, and a heartthrob leading man who always got the girl. And… after a lot of talks with some of the big names in the industry and ready to put his career on the line for something he felt was so important, sometimes Marcus got the boy instead. He was the poster child for success in many, many ways.

Now, nine at night, he was standing in front of the building he'd practically grown up in, and he wasn't sure what to do with himself.

Choi's Taekwondo Academy.

In complete contrast to what he'd built a career on, at ten Marcus had been so shy he could barely talk. He'd kept to himself, had no friends, and hid when his parents had people over. His aunt, who trained herself, had recommended starting him in a martial art. "It builds confidence," she'd said. "It's great exercise. He'll get to meet kids his own age in a different setting."

Still, that first day on the mat, he'd nearly thrown up. Especially with how loud it was, how much was going on, how many people there were.

And then Master Choi had come over and crouched down and smiled at him.

Taemin Choi, barely twenty at the time, was the son of Grandmaster Ki-hyuk Choi, who owned and ran the school. He worked under his father as an instructor and was being groomed to run the school himself. He probably hadn't expected to gain a shadow in the form of a tiny, overwhelmed ten-year-old, but he'd taken it in stride. He was always patient, always kind, and he didn't just teach Marcus and go on his way. He took extra time to go over things, always listened when Marcus talked about an interest of his own, and even scheduled private classes, free of charge, to gently introduce Marcus to sparring. He was the perfect mentor and had entered Marcus's life at exactly the right moment.

Over the five years that Marcus trained at Choi's, Taemin pushed Marcus to be his best. Marcus credited his success as both an actor and a martial artist, the discipline and training and confidence, all to Choi's and to Taemin. Even after moving to California when he was fifteen, even when he started training at different schools and in different disciplines, Marcus stayed loyal. He never wore the patches of any other school, always made sure to practice the Choi forms along with the other ones he learned over the years, and whenever he needed an extra boost, he recited the tenets of taekwondo in his head.

It had crossed Marcus's mind dozens of times to reach out, try to reconnect with Master Choi, but in the end he never could bring himself to do it. What would he say? How would he say it?

What if… what if Master Choi didn't even remember him?

But now, ten years later, wildly successful and still with this gratitude in mind, Marcus was back in Michigan for a shoot.

And Choi's was right there.

He'd planned it out, actually. Had looked up their operating hours online to make sure he wasn't showing up during classes. First off because he hadn't wanted to accidentally cause a scene, being a well-known celebrity. Secondly because he still wasn't quite sure what to *do*. So he'd planned to go over after hours, at least stand in front of the building he loved so much. Look at it, breathe deep, and maybe get the courage to call the next day.

Things had mostly worked out. Classes were clearly over.

But the lights were still on, and there was a man on the mat, and ten years felt like no time at all.

THERE WAS a man standing outside of Taemin's dojang.

Classes had been over for about half an hour. Taemin had said goodbye to his students, gone over his bookwork for the evening, and was wiping down the mats when the man showed up. Taemin had expected him to come in, maybe inquire about lessons, but instead he just… stood there.

Surely he realized, while he could see Taemin through the windows, Taemin could see him as well? It was a dojang. The entire front wall was clear glass.

It might've been a little suspicious all told, but Taemin wasn't too worried. He seemed nervous, but not hostile. Dressed lightly for spring in a thin long-sleeved shirt and dark jeans, he was shifting from foot to foot. He'd take a step and then stop. Take a deep breath and then let it out.

Puzzled, Taemin finished with the mop and set it aside before going over to the door and pushing it open.

The man had clearly seen him, and he looked almost afraid when Taemin stepped outside.

"Hello," Taemin said, with what he hoped was a welcoming smile on his face. "It's a nice night."

"Y-yeah."

He watched the man swallow. Dark, curly hair, a sharp nose—the man looked very familiar, even though for some reason Taemin was remembering much less broad shoulders, a much smaller build.

But mostly he looked nervous. "Is there something I can do for you? Are you interested in lessons, maybe? You're free to come in."

"I—" The man took a step forward and then stopped. Clenched his fists and then relaxed his hands. "I, no, it's okay. It's late, sorry—"

Taemin held out a hand. "It's fine. You sound a little like you need to talk." He paused. The voice, it was deeper, but the cadence of the words, especially said haltingly…. "Do I…." He wracked his brain. It was right there, if only he could put his finger on it. "I'm sorry, but do I know you?"

A sharp exhale, and then the man rubbed the back of his neck, ducked his head. "Um, yeah. Though it—it was a long time ago, I doubt you remember me—"

It hit him all at once. "Marcus?" Taemin asked, eyes widening. "Marcus Economidis?"

Marcus gave him a lopsided grin. One Taemin recognized. The same grin he'd done his best to pull out of a promising but unconfident student. "Hi, Master Choi."

Taemin laughed with delight. "It's been years! How have you been?"

Marcus shrugged, but he was still grinning. "Pretty good."

"Keeping up with your training?" he asked, maybe teasing just a little.

Marcus chuckled. "Yeah I—yeah. You could say that."

"I'd love to catch up with you. Would you like to come in? Just for a little while, maybe."

Marcus ducked his head. "Yeah I'd… I'd really like that, if it's okay with you."

Taemin smiled and held open the door. "Of course it is. Come on in."

MARCUS HAD been fifteen the last time he'd set foot in Choi's dojang. Fifteen when he'd last seen Master Choi—and even then, the last couple of years training with him, Marcus had known his feelings had started to evolve from the basic hero worship to something more.

Taemin hadn't changed much since Marcus had last seen him. Still lean, strong, and incredibly graceful. Still with the same short black hair, the same… god, the same beautiful smile.

The biggest difference was Marcus. He wasn't a gangly five-foot-six teenager anymore. He'd grown into himself, pushing his limits and his body, and now was a solid and strong man. Six two, and at least four inches taller than Master Choi. It was a little disconcerting to be looking down at him instead of up.

He wasn't quite shaking when he followed Master Choi into the dojang, bowing instinctively toward the mat and the flag as he stepped inside. He immediately toed off his shoes and nudged them into sitting neatly side-by-side on the carpeted area in front of the mat. When he looked up, it was to see Master Choi watching him and looking unbearably fond.

Marcus swallowed and smiled back.

"You've remembered all your good habits," Master Choi said, sounding pleased as he led Marcus to the little office off to the side of the mat.

"Well, you know," Marcus said as he sat in the chair Master Choi gestured him to, "I had a really good teacher." Master Choi grinned, and Marcus went hot. "It's really good to see you again, Master."

Taemin shook his head. "We're not training right now. You're a friend coming back into my life. I'm pretty sure you can call me by my first name."

Right. Yeah. Equal footing. Marcus *wasn't* fifteen anymore. And while Master Choi was always going to be Master Choi a little in his heart, right now he was Taemin too. "Taemin, then," Marcus said, trying to shove down some of the anxiety-inducing awe. He was a grown-ass adult. He could handle the fact that he was being treated like one. "It's still good to see you."

"I can say the same. How are you? What are you doing here? I'm certainly not complaining, but it… it's been a long time."

"I know. I'm sorry, I kept… wanting to reach out, but every time I thought to, I couldn't…." He sighed. "I'm sorry."

"Don't be sorry," Taemin said. "Sometimes it's hard to bridge a gap, once the distance has been made. You're here now, and I couldn't be happier. So? What brings you to town?"

"I'm here for a movie shoot." That was an easy, comfortable topic. "We're filming in downtown Detroit. I'm here for at least six months, maybe more than that, depending on how things go."

Taemin's eyebrows shot up. "You're an actor?"

"Yeah." Marcus grinned. He was proud of himself and how far he'd come. And it was a little funny to hear Taemin sound so surprised. "Turns out all your lessons about self-confidence really paid off."

"Really!" Taemin leaned forward. "Please, tell me more."

Still grinning, Marcus launched into the story he knew would make Taemin smile: how his new martial arts school in California had a guest come in and ask about using the location for a short film, how she'd asked some of the students (and parents) permission to use them as extras. How much Marcus had liked it, how he'd decided to try his hand at an acting class after that.

"My teacher was impressed by the martial arts," he told Taemin. "And one day she gave me the name of a talent agency and told me to call them and tell them that she had referred me to try out for the role of Daniel in *Billy's Prayer.* The agency signed me that day and then sent me out on the audition the next. It was this crazy whirlwind, but… one thing sort of led to another."

"That's amazing. I'm so proud of you."

"Thanks. Yeah. I know, it was a big change to go from 'unable to meet anyone's eyes' to being a leading man, but… I owe a lot of it to you."

Taemin huffed a laugh. "I think this is the part where I'm supposed to say it was inside of you all along. And it was! But I know I helped open you up a little, and I'm happy to take the credit when you're clearly so willing to give it to me." He winked, and Marcus couldn't help but laugh. It was so *Taemin.* He hadn't changed one bit. "But speaking of—you did say you were keeping up with your training, didn't you?"

Marcus grinned, took a breath, and rattled off the ten principles of Choi's taekwondo as fast as he physically could. It was something all the kids tried as a personal challenge: reciting the principles in one breath. "—and ten is finish what you start, sir!" He wasn't quite panting when he added, "As if I could ever forget."

Taemin looked absolutely delighted. "You know, a lot of our students have to drop the honorifics in order to say the principles that fast."

Marcus waved a hand. "I've had a lot of practice."

"I'll bet."

"And I've been, you know, keeping up physically too. I do almost all my own fights and stunts on camera. But, uh, off camera I make sure I'm doing things right."

"I'd expect nothing less," Taemin said warmly.

"What about you?" Marcus asked, clearing this throat. "And how is Grandmaster Choi?"

"He's doing well. Very well. He's been much more hands-off the academy for the last few years and mostly comes in for testings and special training sessions and classes. He and my mother spend a lot of time back running their dojang in Korea, now that I'm pretty firmly running the Michigan school."

"Oh wow. So you're leading the entire school yourself?"

"Well, not entirely by myself," Taemin said. "I've got junior instructors to help me with nearly every class. And remember Mr. Avi?" Mr. Avi'd been around only at the tail of Marcus's time at Choi's, but Marcus had been a junior instructor around that time. He was an older man, midfifties when Marcus left. He had to be in his sixties now.

"Yeah, yeah, he's doing well?"

Taemin chuckled. "He's a third-degree and Master Instructor now. Preeti is also an instructor here. You remember her? She was only about ten when you left."

"Hey, yeah! I remember. Preeti. She was 'pret-ty' small. She teaches here now?"

"Yes. She started working as an assistant instructor at seventeen. Now she helps me run classes three nights a week. She even decided to go to college locally so she could continue to work and train here."

"Wow! That's… that's really amazing." Choi's touched so many lives. Was continuing to do so. "What's she going to college for?"

"Sports medicine, actually." Taemin grinned. "So we'll have her around for a while yet."

"That's so cool. Good for her."

"You're welcome to tell her yourself, if you'd like to pay a visit during our open hours," Taemin said. "I'm sure everyone would get a kick out of seeing you."

Marcus raised an eyebrow. "A kick? Really?"

Taemin let out a burst of laughter. "I didn't even do that on purpose, I promise."

God, he was just—if there was a human version of the word *delightful*—"Well," Marcus said, sitting back in his chair, "it's good to know you only make terrible jokes on accident."

"Hey, you show me some respect."

"Yessir."

Taemin laughed again, and Marcus felt himself go warm. He'd missed this. He'd missed *him*.

And Marcus wasn't fifteen anymore.

"Look," he said, "it's late. And I'm sure you've had a long day. I don't want to keep you any longer tonight. But I'd love to keep catching up with you, if you'd be willing."

"Of course I am."

"Awesome. I'm free for the few days while other people get flown in and settled and sets finish being built. I just came in early because I wanted"—*to revisit this place, to check out the changes, to see you again*—"to, you know, get a feel for being back in the D. I—would you like to meet for coffee or something tomorrow? Or it doesn't have to be tomorrow, you know, whenever it works in your schedule."

Taemin tilted his head, considering. "I've got a better idea, if you really are free."

"Yeah?" Marcus asked, trying not to sound too eager.

"I'm here every morning to train. My morning sparring *classes* are Mondays and Wednesdays, but since tomorrow is Thursday, I'll be by myself. I'd be very interested to have a match or two with you. If you're up for it."

Oh my god yes *please*. "Sure. You'd have to lend me some sparring gear, though. I didn't bring mine with me."

Taemin grinned. "I think I can find something to fit you."

"Then yeah, of course. Maybe uh… maybe I could treat you to breakfast afterward?"

"I'd love that."

"Awesome. Okay." Marcus stood up. "Then I'll see you tomorrow. What time?"

"Why don't we say nine. Give us both a little more time to sleep."

Marcus glanced at his watch. Holy shit, it was almost eleven. "Oh man, I'm so sorry I kept you so late. You probably haven't even eaten dinner—" No one trained or taught classes on a full stomach.

Taemin held up a hand. "Please, it's fine. I'm thrilled I got the chance to talk to you. And I look forward to seeing you tomorrow at nine. Okay?"

"Okay."

"Come on. I'll close up here and walk you out."

Once outside the dojang, now with the lights off and the door locked, Taemin turned to Marcus as they neared their parked cars.

"So," he said, holding out his arms. "I don't suppose I get a hug, after all this time?"

Marcus didn't quite rush forward into them. He had to lean down just a bit and—enveloped Taemin just a little.

It felt so good to have him in his arms.

He let go and stepped back. "I'll see you tomorrow."

"Have a good night," Taemin said.

"Yeah, you too."

Chapter Two

TAEMIN WAS not, in fact, a morning person.

He was *good* at getting up early and going about his day, and he did so regularly, but early-morning sparring classes were his father's legacy. Taemin upheld them because it was only right, and it was ever more important to live up to the Choi name now that he was in charge of the school. His father was, after all, one of the handful of living tenth-degree black belts in the world. The normally posthumous honor had been awarded while he was alive due to his accomplishments and dedication to both the taekwondo community and the world at large. Choi's might have been Taemin's birthright, but it was built on Ki-hyuk Choi's push to better himself, his students, and society.

Taemin would not change a thing in regards to what Choi's stood for, but he did have to admit, if given half the chance, he would gladly sleep in past sunrise.

Granted, growing up he didn't get that chance a whole lot, what with his parents' training regimen. Sleeping in past seven was still sleeping in. And his body was in the habit now of waking up early. It didn't mean he had to like it.

It was easier, though, with something to look forward to. Seeing Marcus again… seeing what he'd grown up into…. Taemin was so proud of him. Barring how nervous Marcus had seemed last night, he still carried himself with confidence that showed clearly once the man had relaxed a little. And an actor? That was incredible. He'd have to ask Marcus more about it. Maybe get around to actually seeing a movie he was in. That was reason enough to take the time to watch a film. Taemin wasn't all that great at consuming modern media. He was the first to admit that he was terrible about living in the modern age at all. His students and friends made fun of him about it all the time. He barely was able to run the school's Facebook page and website—in fact he didn't; Preeti did that—much less have a Facebook of his own.

It had actually crossed his mind, over the last few years, to maybe try looking Marcus up, see what he was doing now. But he'd never followed through with it. It felt like crossing a boundary, just showing up out of nowhere to go, "Hey, remember me?" He might have been Marcus's teacher once, but people grew and changed and moved. For all he'd known, Marcus had had no interest in reconnecting.

But now here he was. Grown up and obviously happy with himself and what he was doing. Taemin couldn't wait to talk to him more, hear all about what he'd been up to over the years.

And it was nice to know, just as he'd thought about Marcus from time to time, wondering how things were going, that Marcus had thought about him too.

The bell on the door jingled cheerily, and Taemin turned just as he heard Marcus, voice smoother and deeper now, say, "Good morning."

"Good morning." Taemin smiled and took him in as Marcus bowed into the dojang, stepped out of his shoes, and then walked onto the mat. Last night he hadn't really had the chance to *see* Marcus. Not like he could now, in full daylight. So he used a moment to take him in.

He was tall (though that Taemin had certainly noticed yesterday. It was an interesting experience having to look *up* at him) and broad now, muscular in a way that spoke of hard work and heavy training. He had the same mop of dark, curly hair, the same green eyes. The same smile, though it seemed a little less shy now. He was a handsome man.

Taemin cleared his throat. "Well, I'm glad to see you came dressed to work." Marcus was wearing a worn-looking T-shirt and a pair of track pants. Taemin, of course, was in his dobok. He'd brought clothes to change into, for when they went out for breakfast afterward.

"Of course," Marcus said. "I'm pretty much resigned to you running me ragged. But I'll put up a good fight."

"You'd better. I want to see all the ways you've improved."

"I'll do my best."

Taemin grinned and went to grab the sparring gear he'd picked out to fit a build larger than his own. He held it out to Marcus, who took it and started to put it on.

"You don't want to warm up without it?"

Marcus shook his head. "Better to get used to it right away, if I'm going to be fighting with it." He pointed a finger at Taemin. "And who was it that taught me that?"

"Fair enough. You go and get started. I'll be right back."

Marcus nodded and then started on jumping jacks, while Taemin went to his office and to his computer. From there he opened up the sound file he'd kept at the ready and pressed play.

"Eye of the Tiger" came blasting out into the dojang, and Marcus whipped around so fast it was impressive.

"Master Choi!"

Taemin tried to school his face. "Yes?"

"I swear, if you really plan to play that for the full hour…."

Taemin laughed and walked back onto the mat. "No, that was my father's thing, I promise. I just thought you might like the memory." His father was very fond of the song and used to play it on repeat during sparring sessions. Many of Taemin's students had told him that their reaction to hearing the song now was visceral.

Marcus snorted and dropped into push-ups. His form was perfect. "'Like the memory.' Sure. Don't scare me like that."

Taemin did some basic stretches while the music played out. When it was over, the dojang was loud in the new silence. He moved into a middle split stretch, and when he glanced up, it was to find Marcus looking at him in the mirror. "Oh, are you ready?"

"Uh, yeah. Sparring will do the dynamic stretching for me."

"True enough," Taemin said, getting to his feet.

SPARRING WITH Taemin again was a little unreal. In part because Marcus could almost keep up. It was *work* and he was going to be thoroughly exhausted whenever Taemin called time, but even if he was playing defensively, he was still making Taemin block a fair amount, too, instead of him only being able to dodge away.

"Very nice," Taemin said in between hits. "Your stamina is excellent."

"Thanks," Marcus said, and he felt gratified that he didn't sound too out of breath. "I've maybe been working on it a little."

"I can tell. And your blocks are fantastic. Does this mean I can get fancier?"

"I mean, hey, if you want. I'm not gonna say no."

Taemin immediately grinned at him, then did a jump back spinning hook kick so fast that Marcus hadn't even gotten his arms up by the time Taemin's foot tapped him lightly on the head.

Fuck.

"Point to you," Marcus managed. "God you're fast."

"You're not so bad yourself."

Determined to make a good showing, Marcus stepped into Taemin's next move, caught his arm, and then twisted, going for a takedown. Taemin's eyes widened before the man had to go with the motion, and for a second, Marcus thought he'd actually pinned his mentor.

Then Taemin hooked his ankle behind Marcus's own and pulled, the follow-through motion making Marcus let go and fall forward, which gave Taemin enough time to bounce back to his feet. Marcus stood up a second later, in time to block the kick, but even he could tell it was a leading move.

"Okay," he said, tapping out on his chest, "I think you win. You're just doing a teaching spar with me, at this point."

Taemin shook his head. "You're not giving yourself enough credit. We went on for a long time, and you kept up with me no problem."

Well, Marcus thought, glad for his padding—especially his cup, *that depends on your definition of what a problem might be.* "I don't know about that," he ended up saying. "Though I thought I had you with the takedown."

"So did I, for a minute there. It was excellent, if unorthodox. It shows you have a lot of grappling experience. More training?"

Marcus nodded. "The school I train with now, Dragon Martial Arts, does a lot of close-quarter work."

"That's a big leap from taekwondo."

"I know. I love both styles, so I do my best to train as much as I can."

"It shows," Taemin said. He clapped Marcus on the shoulder. "You're excellent. If you're willing, I'd really like to see you demonstrate some of your takedowns."

"What, now?"

"Sure. You know I'm always up for learning something new. And we're both already here."

"I… yeah." Marcus kept his breathing steady. He could absolutely handle rolling around on the mat a little. This wasn't a big deal. "Yeah, sure. Anything in particular you want to see?"

"Pick a favorite! Surprise me."

Marcus turned some moves over in his head. "All right," he said when he'd settled on one. "Rush me?"

Taemin immediately surged forward, and Marcus stepped out, grabbing Taemin's arm and pulling him off-balance while he used his foot to sweep his legs. Marcus followed him on the way down, the careful, controlled way he knew to move when he was doing a teaching demonstration, but he kept the strength there so that Taemin couldn't easily get away.

It was over in a breadth of a second, Taemin pinned to the mat while Marcus crouched over him, one hand holding his arm in place while the other pressed into the small of his back.

"So the point is to subdue in this case, not to get away I see," Taemin said from his position on the floor. "But very controlled too—a good way to deal with someone you don't want to hurt while having to be on the defensive. A good choice."

"Thanks," Marcus said, feeling off-kilter. "Um." He shook his head, trying to clear it. Neither of them made to move. "Could you get out of this?" he ended up asking, curious.

"Not in the position I'm in. I don't have the leverage. In a real-world situation, my best bet would be to wait until you relaxed the hold to attack me. It's a pinning move, and it's a good one, but it's limited in the fact that you have to physically hold on to the person you're dealing with." He tapped out on the mat and Marcus quickly let him go, standing up and holding out a hand.

Taemin took it and pulled himself to his feet. "So," he said. "That was a lot of fun."

"Yeah." Marcus grinned. It'd been a blast. "Think you worked up an appetite for breakfast?"

Taemin laughed. "Let's get changed and then we can go." He started to take off his sparring gear and Marcus did the same. Once the gear was put away, Taemin headed to the academy's storage room/changing area, and Marcus grabbed up the duffel he'd brought and went into the family-style restroom.

He stripped down and gave himself a cursory wipe with a towel before he applied his deodorant and started to get dressed. He'd head home to shower after breakfast, and he was pretty sure Taemin would do the same. He couldn't help but smile at the knowledge that Taemin would probably also be taking a nap too. He'd often said, all those years ago, that he wasn't a big fan of mornings. And with the school open late since that was when classes took place, he usually took some time in the afternoon to catch up on a little sleep, in between errands and eating and doing things for the academy. If things really hadn't changed all that much, Taemin also spent hours of his time every day volunteering with Kids Kicking Cancer, doing privates with special needs children and adults, and running the midday exercise program he had started with his dad for the local homeschool co-op.

"It keeps my days full," he'd said, when Marcus had asked about the fact that Taemin seemed to have no free time. After he'd graduated college, he only seemed to get busier. He'd always made time for Marcus, though.

Still was, considering today.

Taemin was already out and dressed by the time Marcus emerged from the bathroom. He was wearing jeans and a fitted T-shirt, a big change from the dobok he'd been in yesterday and minutes ago. The day clothes emphasized the lean lines of him.

God, Marcus really needed to get a grip.

"Ready?" he asked as he made his way over to his sneakers and bent to put them on.

"Yep." Taemin was already wearing his shoes. "Where are we headed? Should I follow you?"

"It's up to you. We could just take my car, if you didn't mind my having to drive you back."

"Works for me. Why run two engines when you only need to run one?"

They made their way over to Marcus's long-term rental, Marcus unlocking the door so they both could get in. He had a place in mind and it wasn't too far away, so it was only about ten minutes later that Marcus pulled up in front of an Original Pancake House.

Taemin, as Marcus had hoped, smiled. "This certainly brings back memories."

"It definitely does for me," Marcus said as they got out. "We have these in California, but I uh, I don't get out to it much." The one he'd gone to as a teenager had a really open layout. Once he'd gotten more popular he had been approached so much he sort of lost his taste for the place. But this one was all good memories.

"Shame," Taemin said, shaking his head. "I'm sorry you've been missing out."

"I know, right? It's been forever since I've had a dutch baby." Essentially an inverted pancake filled with powdered sugar and lemon juice, the dutch baby had been Marcus's go-to order at OPH for literal years.

As Taemin knew, if he remembered. They hadn't gone out to eat all that often, what with their respective schedules of Marcus being in school and Taemin essentially living at the academy in between college classes, but some summer mornings, after sparing, Taemin had taken Marcus to the Original Pancake House as a treat. Maybe it was dumb of Marcus to keep reminiscing, but at least it didn't seem as though Taemin minded.

The wait wasn't too bad, since they hadn't arrived at a peak time. Soon enough they were being shown to a booth, sliding in across from each other. They both asked for water, Marcus ordering a coffee as well, and then took a minute to peruse the menu.

Well, Taemin did. Marcus, after all, already knew what he wanted. In more ways than one.

Which was a thought he didn't need to have in a semicrowded restaurant across from the man who had literally been his first crush. A lot of time had passed. They were both older and had changed and grown. Marcus was definitely a different person than he was at fifteen. While he couldn't imagine Taemin at thirty-six was all that different from Taemin at twenty-five, it was *possible.* And either way, that wasn't the point. He was here now to show a mentor and friend how much he'd accomplished—in part thanks to said friendship. To catch up with Taemin, hopefully make him proud (Marcus was able to admit that), and anything else, well….

He was probably being stupid. For all he knew, Taemin was currently in some sort of relationship. Happily married. Would never be interested in Marcus regardless. Their relationship in the past had been mentor-mentee and, of course, completely platonic—even if fifteen-year-old Marcus certainly hadn't wanted it to be.

He was being stupid.

Knowing that didn't change anything.

AFTER A lot of dithering, Taemin ended up ordering the dutch baby treat—a version of the dutch baby that replaced the powdered sugar and lemon with strawberries and bananas. Once their waitress had left their table, he gave Marcus a rueful smile. "Sorry about taking forever to order."

Marcus chuckled. "You say that as if I'm not used to it from you."

"Hey! It's been a decade. For all you know, I'm lightning-fast at ordering food now."

Marcus raised an eyebrow. "Except for right now?"

Taemin laughed. "Except for always. Never mind. So! This movie. What's it about?"

"It's a sci-fi dystopian thing. The general gist of it is that I'm a space-rat, surviving in a beaten-up ship by scrounging around. And I pull this kid out of a trash heap basically. She doesn't remember who she is at first. And I'm sort of this hardened guy, but she's just a kid, you know? I feel sorry for her and kinda take her under my wing a little."

"I'm sure you make a very good space mentor." Taemin grinned. "Then what?"

Marcus drummed his fingers on the table. "Uh, let's see… okay, so we're out one day, stopping off on this planet to pick up some supplies, and her picture's on a wanted poster. And like, she's nine. I'm thinking, what the hell? Turns out she's the daughter of some resistance leaders. She'd been kidnapped to get leverage over her parents, but she'd managed to escape, which is when I found her."

"Okay, okay. And then?"

"We end up meeting up with her brother, who's been looking for her on the down-low. That's the romantic side-plot, by the way." Said casually, it took Taemin a moment to register what Marcus had really just told him, and by then Marcus was continuing, "And the three of us sort of continue on this adventure to basically overthrow the government. It's a bit open-ended, which means there's room for a sequel if things take off. And, you know, it's gritty, but also in a campy way? Like I don't think we'll be taking ourselves too seriously while we film it. I think it'll be fun. And I've worked with Roger before."

"Roger?"

"He'll be playing the brother. He's had a couple smaller roles on a few things I've worked on. This'll be his first *big* big-screen thing. I'm pretty excited for him. Anita, his girlfriend, about died when he told her. She's already made me promise to make sure we have a good blooper reel."

"Wow," Taemin said after what he hoped wasn't too long a moment. "That sounds like it'll be a fun project. And um… I hope this is okay to say, but I'm…." He shifted in his seat. How was he supposed to say how much a male movie star having a male love interest meant to him? With Marcus being one half of that duo, was it better or worse to say something? "I'm just as bad at media as I was ten years ago."

Marcus grinned. "Yeah?"

Taemin nodded. "And so I… I haven't heard much about movies, especially noncontemporary movies, where the main romance isn't…."

"Does it bother you?" Marcus asked, sounding hesitant.

"No! No, not—just the opposite. It's pretty amazing. And it's nice to see it normalized. That it *isn't* a big deal."

Marcus nodded, looking relieved. "Yeah, uh, I fought pretty hard to be able to work on scripts that didn't have a completely heterosexual dynamic."

"That's… well, that's incredibly impressive. You're doing a good thing." Taemin's gaze flickered down to the table. "I'm sure you already know that and don't need to hear it from me, but—"

"No, no, I—thank you." Marcus curled his fingers around his coffee mug. "It means a lot to me that you think so."

They drifted into silence. It wasn't uncomfortable, but it was loud.

"So," Taemin said after a moment, nudging Marcus under the table with his foot, "you promised Roger's girlfriend a blooper reel, hm?"

Marcus sat up a little straighter and smiled. "Oh yeah. I'm thinking that when we have our passionate kiss at the end, I might drop him during a take."

Marcus had obviously meant Taemin to picture something funny, but the image that sprang into his mind was one of Marcus holding someone—a man—and kissing him. It was startling in its clarity. And—what? Where did that even come from? "Maybe don't drop him," Taemin managed. "It's probably bad form to hurt your coworkers."

Marcus laughed, rich and deep. Taemin wasn't going to get tired of hearing that sound anytime soon. "You're probably right. I'll have to brainstorm about what else I can do."

"I'm sure Anita will appreciate your efforts. Though what about you?"

"Me?"

Taemin nodded. "Do you have anyone special in your life right now?"

Marcus went quiet, and Taemin immediately worried. "I'm sorry if that crosses a line. Of course you don't have to talk about that with me if you won't want to."

"No," Marcus said hurriedly. "It's fine. And no, not at the moment. I've dated off and on over the years, but it's never really been anything serious. Just waiting for the right person I guess."

"I'm sure you have the chance to meet all sorts of interesting people in your line of work."

"Yeah, definitely. I've made a lot of good friends." Marcus leaned back in his seat. "I've got some great stunt guys who are usually contracted to work with me. Though we argue a lot about what I want to do for myself. It's all in good fun, though. And I mean, you work for people for months at a time on a project, you're probably going to end up really close or hating each other. I've been lucky enough that it's usually the former over the latter."

"That's great. I'm glad you've got that." It was wonderful to hear about Marcus being surrounded by friends now. He'd been able to open up at Choi's as he'd gotten older, but he'd also *stuck* to Choi's mostly, not really able to take the steps to talk to people at his school. This was a change, but a good one.

"What about you?" Marcus asked.

"What about me?"

"You know. Anyone in your life right now?"

Taemin huffed a laugh. "About five hundred students."

"Really?" Marcus asked, expression unreadable. "No one else?"

Shrugging, Taemin said, "I work long, weird hours. And it's not as if I'm about to go to a bar to try to meet someone."

"Not even through Choi's?" Marcus asked, sounding tentative.

It was nice of him to be so considerate, but the answer to that was easy. "Oh no." Taemin shook his head. "Not while I'm Master Choi. No matter what, my relationship with my students comes with some sort of power dynamic. That's no way to start anything romantic."

"Oh."

"But I keep myself busy," Taemin added. "It's all right." It was lonely sometimes, especially when he was home by himself. Coming back from a long day and… having no one. Sometimes he was exhausted and simply wanted someone to talk to, to curl up with. But his life was full and, for the most part, he was happy. He could deal with loneliness, even if he did hope that one day he wouldn't have to.

Chapter Three

HE MIGHT have been able to keep up an easy conversation through breakfast, but inwardly Marcus's mind was whirling. Taemin was single. That was both great and terrible news. Marcus would have had a much easier time working to keep a lid on how attractive he found Taemin, coupled with his emotional feelings for him, if he'd known he had no chance.

Now, though, he had a glimmer of hope.

He'd been worried, when Taemin had struggled to talk about Marcus's character having a male love interest. He hadn't thought it'd be a big deal at all. After all, Taemin knew Marcus was bi. He'd been one of the first people Marcus had confided in, when he was learning about his own sexuality and struggling with certain aspects of it. Worried about being judged, about being considered a faker, about straight-passing privilege and why some people told him to just *choose*. Taemin had been accepting and compassionate through all of it. Marcus was glad to know his opinions hadn't changed.

And Taemin going on to talk about how much a male-male romance on the big screen meant to him didn't exactly keep Marcus's hopes from growing.

It was fine. He'd... see how things went. He kept having to remind himself that they were both different people now, with new experiences underneath their belts. Besides that, Marcus knew he had a very particular version of Taemin in his head. He couldn't help but look at him through rose-colored lenses.

Even so, Marcus knew he wanted to get to know Taemin again. After meeting him now, he wanted him back in his life, however that happened to be. Everything else would just come as it did.

Right.

Sure.

"We should probably head out," Taemin said ruefully, after their waitress came by yet again to refill coffees and waters. "I think we might have stayed longer than was polite."

"Good point," Marcus said, sliding out of the booth. "And I'm sure you have things to do today, aside from talking to me."

"I'm enjoying talking to you, though," Taemin said with a smile as he got up too. "That's how I lost track of time in the first place."

"Would you like to meet up again?" Marcus asked, snagging the check. And trying not to sound too eager.

"I'd love to. What is your schedule like?"

"I told you, I'm pretty free for the next few days. My PA, Billy, doesn't even get in until Sunday night."

"PA?"

"Personal assistant. I've worked with Billy for about three years now. He's great. Really makes sure my life runs smoothly." Including booking Marcus an early flight into Michigan and coordinating with the film's producer so Marcus could get settled in his short-term apartment before the rest of the cast arrived. He hadn't even asked too many questions—not that he needed to. Marcus hadn't exactly kept much from him when he'd learned the filming location. Billy was two years older than Marcus to the day, and Marcus, twenty-two and tired, hadn't really believed that some guy around his age would have been as good as Billy was. That opinion had certainly changed.

"Oh, I see. Very interesting. As for that, then, well… the invitation to come to classes sometime this week still stands."

Marcus nodded before he turned to pay, thinking about it. Once he stowed the receipt in his wallet, he said, "I wouldn't mind seeing Preeti and Mr. Avi again."

"Technically, if we're going for honorifics now, it's 'Ms. Preeti' and 'Master Avi,'" Taemin said with a grin. "Though I'm pretty sure they'll both tell you that you're being ridiculous. Especially Preeti. Then again, I can't call him anything but 'Mr. Avi,' so I think it's your call."

"I'd love to see Preeti call me ridiculous. I'm sure Preeti now is kinda different from Preeti when she was ten."

Taemin pinched his fingers together. "Just a bit."

As they were leaving the restaurant, two teenage girls ran up to them. "Um, I'm so sorry, excuse me, um," one of them said. "But are—are you, um, are you—"

"Oh my god, Sarah," the other one hissed, before saying to Marcus, "You're—you're Marcus Economidis, right?"

Marcus glanced at Taemin before turning to them, all smiles. "Yeah. Hi there."

"Oh my god. Oh my god." Not-Sarah pulled out her phone. "I—sorry, can we get a picture?"

"Sure," Marcus said easily.

"Oh, I could take it," Taemin said, holding out a hand.

Not-Sarah gave him her phone, and the three of them posed while Taemin took a few different shots, holding the phone out to not-Sarah when he was done. "How's that?"

"Perfect," she breathed, staring at the screen.

"Thank you so, so much," actually-Sarah said, voice wobbling. She looked a little like she was about to start crying. Marcus hoped she didn't. He didn't *mind* it when fans cried, per se, but it was always a little awkward and uncomfortable. "I love your movies. Oh my god."

"Thanks," Marcus said. "I really appreciate the support. You both have a good day now, okay?"

The girls nodded frantically, and Marcus took the opportunity to keep walking to his car, Taemin close behind him.

"Sorry about that," Marcus said as they got in. He was kind of embarrassed. He had fans come up to him often enough that it wasn't startling anymore, but he wasn't sure how Taemin would feel about Marcus getting fawned over by two random teenagers.

"Does that happen a lot?" Taemin asked, curious.

"Uh, some." Marcus started his car and pulled out of the parking lot. "It's weird. You'd think that it'd happen more often in California, but I'm recognized more when I'm filming at other locations. I think it's because people know to look for me?"

"Does it bother you?" Taemin asked. "Having so many people… know who you are like that?"

"It's okay. I like it more than I dislike it. Not the attention but—being who I am, I can really mean something to people. That means everything from making an anti-bullying statement on Twitter to doing a Make-A-Wish appearance."

"That's pretty noble."

Marcus flushed. "Not really. It's just something I can do. Someone I can be for other people. I… you know. I was lucky that I had some really positive influences right when I needed them." *Like you,* he didn't say. "If I can do my own part in helping other people out, I want to do that."

Taemin nodded thoughtfully. "Yes. Noble." He smiled. "I was right the first time."

Marcus cleared his throat. "So, uh, yeah, I'd be down to swinging by the dojang tonight."

"Tonight?" Taemin sounded surprised.

"I mean, if you're not sick of me yet," Marcus quickly amended.

"No, no, please come. I'm sure everyone will be excited to see you." A short pause. "In more ways than one, considering how well-known you seem to be."

"I was going to ask about that," Marcus said. "I think it might be better if I came in at the end of classes, you know? I don't want to, like, make a scene by accident, in case some of your students recognize me."

"That's a good point. Okay, well, the four thirty class is our kid's class, and the five thirty and six thirty classes are family-style. The seven thirty class is adults only, if you wanted to come to that one? Preeti and Mr. Avi will both be there today. Or if you didn't want to actually attend the class, it's over at eight thirty, so you could come around then to at least say hello."

"I don't want to disrupt the class," Marcus said. "But I would like to see you again, and see them. I could do eight thirty. Maybe a little after that, just to give your students some time to leave?"

"Sure, please do come by. I'd love to see you again so soon. And Preeti and Mr. Avi will be in for a treat."

"Okay," Marcus said. "I'll be there."

They said goodbye at Choi's. Taemin disappeared inside, presumably to get his own things, and Marcus headed over to the short-term apartment complex he was being put up in for the duration of filming.

Once he was "home," he emptied his workout clothes into the laundry bin and stripped down to jump in the shower. As he methodically soaped himself up, his mind wandered. Tonight. He'd be seeing Taemin again tonight. *I'd love to see you again so soon.* Of course it was said platonically, but Marcus could dream.

Fuck it, he was a grown-ass man. While Taemin had said he took issue with dating students (which did, Marcus had to admit, make some sense regardless of how old a student might be), Marcus wasn't a student anymore. Taemin was single, attractive, and interesting. They already knew each other. Kind of. Had a history. It wasn't weird that Marcus liked Taemin now, old enough to really be able to act upon it. If Taemin wanted.

Christ, he knew he was going in circles. Though it was honestly a little hilarious how knotted up he was about this; this was the type of stuff that went on in his movies all the time.

Then again, according to *those* scripts, he was absolutely supposed to follow his heart and make a play for his guy. He made a living off wooing people, and he certainly knew how to apply those skills where they mattered.

He was wealthy. He knew he was attractive. For the next few days, he also had nothing but time. There was nothing stopping him from asking Taemin out on a date except himself.

And the fact that doing so literally twenty-four hours after meeting him for the first time in ten years was probably a bit much.

Okay, so he'd wait a week to ask about an actual date. And use that time to scope things out, too, see if he *should* do the asking, as opposed to leaving well enough alone.

"MASTER CHOI, is everything okay?"

Taemin looked up from where he was cataloging the day's attendances. As usual, he had been thinking about why he didn't simply bring in a computerized check-in system, like so many other schools did now. But his father had taught him this method, his students were used to it, and if nothing else, he really was abysmal with technology. "Of course, Preeti. Why?"

Preeti shrugged from where she was standing in the office doorway. "No reason. You just usually aren't in here this long, for the last class." Which was true. Taemin ran the adult class himself, but if he really couldn't for some reason, he at least popped in and out: overseeing Mr. Avi and Preeti, correcting stances, giving advice, talking to the students. But today he had everyone bow in and then retreated to his office, intent on getting his evening paperwork done so when Marcus came by, he'd be able to spend more time with him.

He had to grin at Preeti. "I'm a little bit set in my routines, huh?"

She raised an eyebrow. "Sir, I've seen your schedule. You allot for practically every minute."

She wasn't wrong. "Oh?"

Preeti nodded. "And you do attendances after everyone bows out for the night. We chat until the class leaves, and then we all put away the bags. We don't need to sweep or mop, because I sweep Mondays, and Mr. Avi sweeps Wednesdays before you mop Wednesday night, and then I do social media and stuff while you do attendances. And sometimes Mr. Avi stays to talk."

"Someone's been paying attention."

"Yep. So? What's going on?"

Taemin smiled at her. "You'll find out soon enough."

"Uh. Okay. Good news?"

"You could say that."

"Oh! Does it have anything to do with your upcoming tournament?" The taekwondo national championship tournament for Olympic qualification was coming up in about a month. Taemin was competing and had been doing a lot of additional training and traveling to prepare for it.

Taemin shook his head. "Nothing like that. You'll just have to see."

Preeti sighed. "Fine." She glanced over her shoulder. "Looks like it's time to bow out."

Taemin stood up and followed her out of the office. The evening sparring had finished, and Mr. Avi was conducting the cool down.

"*Gyeongrye*!" Mr. Avi commanded when he caught sight of him. The class bowed in respect to Taemin as he bowed onto the mat, and he walked to the front of the class, underneath the flag, to conduct bow-out.

Just as he led the command and finished the class with everyone reciting the tenets of taekwondo, the bell over his door jingled.

He turned to greet Marcus, who was bowing into the building.

Taemin quickly strode over to him. "You made it!"

"I said I would." Marcus grinned down at him. "Hey."

Taemin, a naturally tactile person, held out his arms in invitation, and Marcus wasted no time stepping forward into the hug. When they parted, Marcus looked up just in time to see Preeti almost barrel into him. She didn't quite, stopping just before she stepped off the mat.

"Marcus!" she said, pointing to him. "Marcus, right? Economidis?"

"Uh, yeah," Marcus said, looking a little startled. "Preeti?"

"One and the same. Just a little bit older. Oh man, I've been following your stuff for years!" She paused. "I mean, like, not in a creepy way? But, you know, you used to train here and then you got all famous, and it's not like I was going to try to friend you on Facebook or anything, but it was cool to see how you were doing and stuff. So. Uh. Yeah. Hi!"

"Hey," Marcus said again, now grinning. "It's good to see you."

Some of the other students had clearly taken an interest in the newcomer. Preeti and Mr. Avi were the only people who would probably remember or recognize Marcus from when he had trained at Choi's. Most of the other students who attended Choi's around the time Marcus did had moved away like he had, or gone off to school, or had otherwise stopped coming.

"Hell," Mr. Avi said, squinting at their little group. "Did I hear that right? Marcus?"

Marcus turned to him. "Mr. Avi, hey!"

Mr. Avi held out a hand, and Marcus shook. "Man, you've grown up. What are you doing back here?"

"Couldn't stay away," Marcus said easily. "I'm in town for a job."

"Is that right? Here to stay?"

"Oh yeah," Preeti said. "You're filming in Detroit, aren't you? Wayne State's got a Economi-watch on right now, since a lot of film students are applying to work as PAs and runners and stuff."

"A what now?" Mr. Avi asked.

"Economi-watch," Marcus said, shifting where he stood. "Uh, it's basically slang for people keeping an eye out for me."

Mr. Avi frowned. "The hell? Why?"

Marcus rubbed the back of his neck. "I work in the film industry. So, uh—"

Mr. Avi's eyebrows shot up. "Holy shit, you're kidding. You a movie star or something?"

"Kinda, yeah."

"Man, you were so quiet! But that's great. Good for you, kid."

"Thanks." Marcus smiled.

"It's good to see you." Mr. Avi slapped Marcus on the back. "But I've got to get going. Julia's a little under the weather." Julia was Mr. Avi's wife.

"I'm sorry to hear that. I hope she feels better."

"No worries, she'll be right as rain soon. Just a cold with the seasons changing. Am I going to be seeing more of you around here, while you're in town?"

"I'm hoping so. At least for the next few days, since filming doesn't start until then. I just came in early, since I wanted to get a feel for being back in Michigan again."

Mr. Avi nodded. "Makes sense to me. All right, all right, good. You should come in for an actual class, then. Can't have you slacking."

Preeti looked like she was about to combust, Taemin thought with amusement. "Mr. Avi, Marcus—"

"Is absolutely looking forward to trying out a class," Marcus interrupted with a grin.

"Good to hear. Well you have a nice night, okay? And good luck on that economist watch thing."

"Thanks."

Some of the other students came over to see what was going on, and Marcus got recognized by several of them. Not as Marcus the old student, but as Marcus the movie star. He obligingly took a few pictures and signed a few autographs (once Taemin grabbed a permanent marker from his office), but then Taemin politely but firmly ushered his students out.

Eventually it was just him, Marcus, and Preeti.

"I can't believe you're really back," Preeti said, when it was quiet again in the dojang.

Marcus nodded. "For about six months at least. We're turning half of Detroit into a sci-fi dystopia. And there's an infinity room in the area big enough for everything the production team wants."

"What's an infinity room?" Preeti asked.

"It's basically a large white room with curved walls," Marcus replied, making a shape with his hands. "It gives the illusion of going on forever. Really useful for green screen and perspective stuff. I think the one we're going with is normally used for car commercials."

"That's so cool."

"I have an idea," Marcus said. "It's late, but I'd still really like to catch up with you both. Mind if I take you two out to dinner?"

"I'm down," Preeti said immediately.

"Taemin? Is that okay with you?"

"Sure, I'd love to." Taemin nodded at Preeti. "Why don't we both get changed, and then we can go."

"Sounds good," Marcus said.

"Did you have a place in mind to go?" Taemin asked, once they were all changed and ready.

"Would you guys be okay if we did a Coney Island?" Marcus asked, holding up his phone. "They're open pretty late, which is kinda a priority."

"Sure," Preeti said. "I'm ready to order an omelet the size of my face and also probably get a slice of cheesecake." At Marcus's amused look, she said, "What? I'm full-time pre-med, a professional martial artist, and a vegetarian. I'll get my protein where I can."

"I didn't say a thing." Marcus grinned as they made their way to the parking lot.

IT WAS bizarre to see Preeti all grown up. And to hear her talk like, well, not a little kid. But it was cool. And kind of nice to have someone else to talk to about Choi's.

And maybe tease Taemin a bit, because it was clear he and Preeti had that sort of relationship now that she wasn't, you know, a child.

"All right," Marcus said as they slid into a booth, Preeti and Taemin on one side, Marcus on the other. Part of him wished he could sit next to Taemin, but the more logical part knew that sitting across from the both of them would make conversations a lot easier. Besides, Marcus was a large guy. Better not to crowd anyone if he didn't have to. "Remember, my treat, so order whatever you want."

Preeti looked delighted. "Okay, definite yes to the cheesecake, then."

Marcus laughed. "Sounds good to me."

They all took a few minutes to peruse the menus before they each settled on their orders. Preeti, like she'd intended from the beginning, ordered a vegetarian omelet, and so did Taemin in the end. Because it was so late and he wanted something lighter, Marcus ordered a grilled chicken salad.

"Can I ask you a sort of personal but also you're-a-movie-star-related question?" Preeti asked, once the waitress had taken their orders.

"Shoot."

"Do you have a diet plan? Like a fancy one?"

Marcus huffed a laugh. "Not really. Or kind of? I'm really active, so part of my 'diet plan' is mostly to make sure I'm eating enough food. But the type of food also matters. I've got a bit of leeway with junk just because again, I'm active and I'm a big, muscular guy. But mostly I have to make sure my macros are on point. I had an issue a couple years ago when a new nutritionist put me on a plan that had a lot of vegetables. Nothing wrong with veggies, but if they fill you up, you're too full for other foods you might need. Protein especially. We all noticed pretty fast because I dropped weight when I shouldn't have, and reworked my plan. I actually get a lot of veggies in juice and smoothie form now, because the calories don't change but the density does, so I can eat more. But yeah, same as anyone really; eat a good balance of proteins, fats, and carbs, and fruits and vegetables are good for you." He paused. "Sorry, that was probably more information than you cared about."

"No way, that's really interesting! And it's great that you're paying attention to that. I mean, I told you I'm pre-med, right?"

Marcus nodded. "Taemin mentioned sports medicine?"

"Yeah. So, I mean, nutrition is super important." She tilted her head in Taemin's direction. "For instance. He doesn't eat enough."

"Excuse you, I eat fine," Taemin said, with the air of someone who had had a conversation multiple times.

"What he means is that he gets busy and forgets," Preeti said. "I legit bring him food whenever I'm at the dojang, I stock his office with protein bars and dried fruit and stuff, and he still forgets."

Marcus leveled a look at Taemin. "You seriously didn't get any better in ten years?" To Preeti he said, "He's been like this forever."

"I'll just bet."

Taemin rolled his eyes. "I'm not starving to death."

"He fainted once," Preeti told Marcus.

"Taemin!" Marcus said with horror. "When? Why?"

"Honestly," Taemin grumbled. "It was once. I've been alive almost thirty-six years. I fainted *once.* And my entire school won't let me forget it."

"Maybe if it hadn't been right after you won sparring nationals two years ago," Preeti said. "You know, that thing that literally everyone was paying attention to."

"Wait," Marcus said, "What?"

Preeti nodded. "Oh yeah. He got gold, bowed to his competition, the committee, and then collapsed during commentary. Medical said it was low blood sugar."

"No one eats before competition," Taemin insisted. "It was just an off day."

"Yeah, no," Marcus said. "I'm with Preeti. I know how much I have to eat to get through a day. You work harder than I do and I'm gonna heavily doubt that you eat as much as you should."

"Well I'm eating now," Taemin huffed. "So we can move on to the next topic of conversation."

"Okay, okay," Preeti said. "So, Marcus, I mean, I follow you on Instagram and Twitter and stuff—still not creepy!—but like… how have you been?"

"Pretty good," Marcus said, understanding her question. "I've got a lot of new experiences under my belt now. Some great, some… not so great. But I like my life, I like my work, I like a lot of the people. I really can't complain. What about you?"

Preeti wrinkled her nose. "Oh, I totally can complain. Pre-med is *awful.* Not, you know, enough that I want to quit, but god is it a lot of work."

"And you're training and teaching on top of it," Marcus said. "Full load, there."

"Yeah, but what can you do? I'm not about to compromise on any of it. My grades are good, which is what really matters to my parents. And they're proud of what I've done with martial arts."

"What dan are you now?"

"Just second."

Fiction / General / Lit. Fic, NEC

Fiction / Gen / African Amer.

Fiction / Romance / Gen / Rippy

II. License Types & Limits

Applicants can determine the type of license they marijuana business they want to operate. For exai at least four (4) different options depending on wl market and how they want to operate their busine

"'Just second' nothing," Taemin said. "That's a lot of hard work involved in any belt rank."

Preeti shrugged good-naturedly. "Yessir."

"Also you have one more testing to get your last star, and then it's third-degree for you." Taemin rubbed his hands together. "You're going to hate me."

"I know," Preeti moaned. "It is going to be the actual worst day."

"Two days," Taemin said with a grin. "Third-degree and up, the test usually lasts two days."

"Oh my god."

"Oh hush. I'm testing for sixth next year. You don't see me complaining."

"Wow," Marcus said, impressed. "I'm not surprised that you're going for sixth dan soon, but wow."

Taemin threw him a grin. "It helps when you've been studying at the same place and under the same man since *before* being born."

"Point."

When their food arrived, Marcus launched into a story about his current training regimen to give Preeti and Taemin time to eat. They interspersed chewing with questions, and that turned into another discussion about techniques. Taemin and Preeti's backgrounds were both squarely Korean, while Marcus—though taekwondo would always be his first love—had dabbled in a lot of different styles over the years to get as well-rounded (and sometimes as acrobatic) as possible. He was also currently spending a lot of time on Brazilian jiujitsu, after making friends with a Professor who worked as a stunt coordinator on his last movie. Aside from that, all three of them were interested in weapons work, though Taemin and Marcus had more variety under their belts than Preeti.

"I like bo," she said. "And you will pry my collapsible bo staff from my cold, dead hands. But I'm fine with just focusing on that, sparring, and *poomsae*. Especially since I'm also splitting my time with school."

"No, no, that makes a lot of sense," Marcus said. "Why bo?"

By the time they were all done with dessert—Marcus had just ordered cheesecake for the three of them—it was pretty late.

"Oh man," Preeti said as they walked out to their cars. "Class tomorrow is going to suck."

"I tell you every night that you should go to bed earlier," Taemin said.

"And I'm never going to do that," Preeti said solemnly. "I have other things to do. I can sleep when I'm dead. Or at least graduated."

Taemin clucked his tongue. Marcus grinned. "You should take a leaf out of Taemin's book and take naps."

"Oh believe me, I do my best. If I didn't, I would literally be dead already. But regardless, I'm glad I stayed up." She grinned at him. "It was really good talking to you. Mr. Avi was right—you absolutely should come by the dojang more. Even if it's not to take a class, just to hang out before or after. I'm usually there about an hour early on days I teach. Get some homework or training in, etcetera."

"And you're welcome to come by in general," Taemin said. "I think I might've said that already, but I'm going to extend the invitation again."

"I don't want to disrupt your schedule or anything," Marcus said, touched. And already knowing he wanted to spend as much time around Taemin as he could. Preeti was fun too. He'd like to hang out with her more, for sure. "And you told me this morning how busy you are." Taemin had gone into a bit of his weekday schedule at breakfast.

"This morning?" Preeti asked.

"Marcus and I met for a morning spar and then went out to breakfast," Taemin explained.

"I'm so jealous! How did the sparring go?"

"How do you think?" Marcus laughed. "Taemin kicked my ass."

"Only figuratively," Taemin said. "And you had some interesting takedowns. He's very fast."

"We'll have to spar sometime," she said.

"Definitely," Marcus said. "I'd like that."

"But for now, I should really go home and sleep. Thanks for dinner. I'll see you soon?"

"I'll be around. Here, you want my number? We can text. Set up a time to actually have that spar."

"Seriously?" she asked. "Yeah, absolutely." She pulled out her phone, and Marcus gave her his number.

Then Marcus realized—"Taemin, um, I don't have yours, if you wanted to keep in touch? So I wasn't just dropping in on you at the dojang."

"Or showing up when I wasn't there," Taemin said wryly, taking his phone out of his pocket. "Of course. What was your number again?"

Marcus rattled it off a second time, and soon enough his pocket buzzed twice. When he opened it up, he had texts from two new numbers.

Hi! It's Preeti! :)

This is Taemin.

Marcus smiled and saved them both.

Preeti waved goodbye, and then it was just Marcus and Taemin in the parking lot.

"Thank you for taking us out," Taemin said, smiling up at him. "It was nice to see you again so soon."

Marcus's breath caught. "Yeah, of course. I'm really enjoying spending time with you." *Can we do it again?*

"So am I. And Preeti had a good time too." He laughed. "She's about as down-to-earth as it gets, so she might pepper you with questions about your job, but she won't treat you any differently for it."

Marcus grinned. "Yeah, I got that impression." Inwardly he was sighing, though. Preeti was great, but she wasn't the one he was interested in. He was looking forward to seeing her again, but right now he was more concerned with how soon he could see Taemin again without being a bother. The last thing he wanted to do was overstep.

He nodded at their cars. “It is pretty late. And while I don’t have to get up early, I’m sure you do. You should head home.”

“Yeah,” Taemin said. “True.” He sighed. “Is it weird that I don’t want to say goodbye yet, though? It’s been really nice, being with you today.”

“No,” Marcus said in a rush, trying not to sound too eager. “Not weird at all. I feel kinda the same way. Would you maybe like to get together again tomorrow? Or—that might be too soon for you? Saturday?”

“While I’d love to see you Friday, it probably isn’t a good idea,” Taemin said. He sounded disappointed about it. Marcus’s heart leapt. “I’ve been training with some fellow high-ranks on Friday mornings, and tomorrow we’re meeting in Ann Arbor. After that I’ve got some errands to run, and I’ve got the homeschool co-op at one. Then classes start at four thirty, and I teach by myself on Friday nights.”

“That’s a lot,” Marcus said.

“It is,” Taemin said, shrugging one shoulder. “But a lot isn’t necessarily bad. Though it does mean that by the time class is done at seven thirty, I’m about ready to collapse. And Saturday classes start at eight, so Friday evening is mostly just an early night for me.”

“Yeah, no, that makes total sense. Are you sure you’d be up for something on Saturday?”

“Oh yes, absolutely. Did you have something in mind?”

“Hey, you know the area better than I do now. But I’d be just as happy hanging out or helping at Choi’s.”

Taemin laughed. “Don’t say that, or you’ll just end up living there. And it’s probably good for me to get out once in a while.”

“Okay, well, you said classes end at like one, right?”

“Mm-hm. I usually spend another hour or two on the mat myself, then head home to shower.”

Marcus hid a frown. Classes started at eight, went ’til one, and Taemin trained on his own after? That was at least six hours on the mat, and Taemin hadn’t said anything about breaks. No wonder Preeti got on his back. “How about we go out for a late lunch, then? And then see how we feel after.”

"Sure. I'd like that."

Marcus smiled. "All right, sounds like a plan to me. Would you like me to meet you at Choi's?"

Taemin bit his lip, considering, which only made Marcus focus on his mouth. "Only if you want to. You're free to just come by my apartment."

"Uh y-yeah. Yeah, sure. Meet there, and then we'll go to lunch? I can drive."

Taemin nodded, then covered his mouth to yawn. "Sorry, it's been a long day."

"No, no, I totally get it. See you Saturday then?"

"Okay. I'll text you my address."

"All right. Don't run yourself too ragged tomorrow, okay?"

"I'll do my best," Taemin said, amused.

Chapter Four

AFTER MARCUS did his workout in the morning, he used most of Friday to refamiliarize himself with the area. Drove around town looking at places he remembered—or seeing what they'd been turned into. And looking up some different places to eat, depending on what Taemin felt like.

In-between he spent some time on the phone with his agent Wendy, Billy, his mom just to let her know how he was settling in, and Roger, to go over some parts in the script and bounce ideas back and forth. One of the most important parts of any romance was properly portraying the chemistry. Though London, the film's director, would have a big role in that, since he and Roger already knew each other, it didn't hurt to try to figure out different ways they could approach things.

All told it was a good day, busy but still relaxing. It was kind of nice to be away from California *before* he started working. He enjoyed having a bit of downtime, especially knowing what he'd be getting into the next several months. He loved what he did, but man could days get long. And tiring, especially with how physical he was.

At around six, his phone buzzed with an incoming text message. And when he checked it, expecting it to be from someone or something job related, he was pleasantly surprised to find that it was Preeti.

Hey! Just finished with classes for the day. How did the day go for you?

Pretty well, he replied. *Relearning the area. How was class?*

The semester just started and I'm already so ready for it to be over OTL. Papers and presentations are kicking my ass right now.

Sounds rough.

Actually the worst!!

Marcus had to laugh. He really liked what he'd seen of Preeti so far. *Well if you need to get out some energy, I'm still down for that spar.*

The three dots flashing, indicating a message being typed, appeared and disappeared for a few moments before *Wanna go tomorrow? I'm off Saturday at the Academy because Master Choi insisted I have a weekend what with being a college kid, but I'm free. Specialty Training class is from 12-1, so it's usually a smaller group of dedicated people if you were up for it.*

I would, but I'm already meeting Taemin tomorrow when he's done with classes. I don't want to get under his feet too much.

This time the reply was immediate. *Please. He'd probably be delighted. He always is, when people take more of an interest in the sport.*

Marcus was pretty interested all right. There'd be no complaints from him about seeing Taemin sooner. But he'd meant what he said about not wanting to be overbearing about it. *How about I ask him what he thinks and then get back to you?*

Okay, cool. Just let me know!

Will do.

Awesome.

Taemin had classes until seven thirty, but there was no harm in sending out a message now, for him to see when he was finished. He tapped it out and sent it, then decided to go over his script a little more. He liked being off-book as soon as possible, because it made figuring everything else out, like his blocking, the emotions of the scene, a lot easier.

TAEMIN BOWED-OUT his last class, they all said their goodbyes, and then he was able to sigh and let his shoulders sag a little. He was always a little exhausted by Friday evening, which was one of the reasons it was so nice it was an earlier day. His plan was, as usual, to log the attendances for the day, go home, take a shower, eat, and go to bed.

He absentmindedly checked his phone as he was locking up the school for the night, surprised to see that he had a message from Marcus, sent a couple hours ago.

Hey, Preeti invited me for a spar during your 12-1 class tomorrow. Would you mind if I showed up?

Why would he mind? Taemin thought. Of course not. Just the thought of seeing Marcus a little sooner—and training at the academy no less—made something in him brighten. *Like I'm about to say no to seeing you and Preeti spar.*

The reply came only a few seconds later. *As long as you're okay with it. I'll tell Preeti I accept her challenge then :)*

Taemin chuckled. *You're always free to come by, you know. Even if we're not actively open, as long as I'm there you're free to come by. To use the space or just talk, whatever.*

Thank you. I'll keep that in mind. So I'll see you at noon then, if you're sure about tomorrow?

I'm sure, Taemin typed, leaning against the door of his car. *And I'll have that sparring gear ready for you too.*

Thanks.

Have a good night.

You too.

Taemin stowed his phone, got into his car, and drove home. It was nice having a little moment to talk to Marcus after class. It made him feel a bit less bone-tired.

Once he'd arrived at his apartment and flipped on the lights, he stepped out of his shoes and hung up his keys, then went to throw his dobok and underclothes in the laundry before getting into the shower. That never took very long, so he was out, dry, and dressed for bed sooner over later.

Food. He should eat dinner. Preeti and Avi were forever harping on him to eat. He wasn't that hungry, never really was after a long day, but he knew he needed fuel.

He didn't have a whole lot at home (he'd need to go grocery shopping after his time with Marcus), so he ended up making a simple egg dish. Second night in a row for what was basically a veggie omelet, but Preeti was right; protein was important. You had to get it somehow.

Not for the first time, Taemin spared a thought at the fact that he shouldn't let himself be bullied by someone over fifteen years his junior, but Preeti was basically a little sister at this point. She was allowed some leeway.

By the time he'd brushed his teeth, his energy had thoroughly left him. He collapsed into bed. Made sure his alarm was set, then closed his eyes.

His last conscious thought was of how much he was looking forward to seeing Marcus again.

MARCUS BOWED into Choi's just as the 11:00 a.m. class was finishing up. He was already wearing his cup and had brought his mouth guard, which he traveled with everywhere, but the rest of the gear Taemin would supply. He'd worn another set of track pants and an old T-shirt, and a baseball cap pulled low over his eyes. He had no idea if anyone would recognize him, but he sort of hoped no one did. He was liking the anonymity of being able to train at the dojang in peace.

Preeti, Mr. Avi, and Taemin were all on the mat, along with four adults and two guys who looked around their late teens. The class itself was already going while the 11:00 a.m. class packed up, so the specialty training group was probably part of the adult class that had stayed. Preeti was in full sparring gear and going at a bag, while Taemin and Mr. Avi were doing a bo staff drill, most of the class following along.

He stepped out of his shoes and put them in a cubby, then stuffed his drawstring bag and hat in there too.

Mr. Avi caught sight of him first. "Marcus, hey! Good to see you, kid. You coming for class?"

"Yeah. I thought it'd be fun."

"Also he's sparring with me today," Preeti said over her shoulder.

"No kidding? I'm looking forward to seeing that."

"Me too," Taemin said.

"Wait," from one of the teenagers. "He's sparring Preeti? Just like that? I've never seen him before." To Marcus he said, "You're gonna *die.*"

The other teenager elbowed him, "Jamal," he hissed, "don't you recognize him?"

Oh. Sounded like at least one person knew who he was. Oh well. It wasn't like that was atypical. He did action movies. It was fairly expected that people, especially those interested in the fighting arts, would know him.

Jamal squinted at him, and then his eyes widened. "Holy shit."

Marcus opened his mouth, but Mr. Avi got there first. "That gonna be a problem, Jamal? Roshen?"

They quickly shook their heads. "Nosir."

"Good. He's training here today. He's just another student."

"Yessir."

Mr. Avi glanced at Marcus. "Just another student, right?"

Marcus nodded and couldn't help a smile. This was more like it. "Yessir."

"All right. Now then." Mr. Avi turned to the class as a whole. "A black belt is stepping onto the mat!" he bellowed. "Show your respect!"

"Sir!" Everyone bowed to Marcus, then, to their credit, returned to what they were doing before they'd been interrupted. Though most of them still looked over at him in curiosity or recognition.

After nodding to Taemin, Marcus started warming up, watching the class out of the corner of his eye. It was clear they were a dedicated bunch, concentrating hard on the instruction and then doing the repetitions until they were shown the next set of movements. They all, for the most part, moved fluidly—obviously having had trained the form for a while.

When he was good and ready, he went over to stand at the edge of the class in parade rest to wait for Taemin to notice him. It didn't take long.

"Ready?" Taemin asked.

Marcus nodded. "Yessir."

"Great! Let me get your gear." Almost at once, the class stilled in their movements to watch as Marcus padded up. "Do you mind if you have an audience?" Taemin asked.

"Only if Preeti does."

"Are you kidding?" Preeti came over, her long ponytail swinging from where it was hanging out of the top of her helmet. "It'll be more fun this way. Sir? Will you preside?"

"Of course." Taemin motioned to the class, and they all moved to the edge of the mat and took a knee. Roshen in particular looked like he was about to start vibrating with excitement, watching. "Step up!"

Preeti and Marcus stepped forward until they were just in front of Taemin.

"Pad check!" He went over to Preeti, who bowed to him, and then he went up her body from shin-guards to helmet, lightly slapping each pad before instructing her to knock. When he was finished, he turned to Marcus, who bowed as well, and Taemin did the same thing to him. "Knock!" Marcus knocked, proving that he was wearing a cup, too, and Taemin nodded.

"Face each other." They did. "*Charyeo*!" They both stood at attention. "Gyeongrye!" They bowed to each other. "*Sijak*!" Begin. They fist-bumped, then began to bound back and forth, circling as the match started.

Two minutes was a long time for constant movement, and Preeti kept Marcus on his toes. Figuratively and literally. She was fast and agile, and he spent just as much time blocking and dodging as he did on offense, learning her moves.

Marcus got first points, a headshot, and he grinned at Preeti around his mouth guard before bringing up his hands just in time to block a truly impressive jump spin kick.

When Taemin called time, they were both breathing hard but smiling wide, excited over the match and their own showing. Taemin awarded Marcus the first match before starting the second round.

More movement, heart pounding, heat-of-the-moment strikes and blocks. Three points to Preeti for a to-the-head roundhouse that got in around Marcus's guard, three points to Marcus for body-blows in quick succession. When time was called, Preeti was awarded the match.

"Last one," Taemin said, before instructing them to bow and get into ready stance. "Sijak!" They fist-bumped and the final round began.

By this time they'd each learned a little bit about the other's fighting style and they went at it, each giving it their all, no tiptoeing around trying to feel things out. Marcus managed to get the upper hand, playing offensive and forcing Preeti to pull out block after block. She dropped her elbow, a signal that she was gearing up for another spin kick, and Marcus dove in to take a shot, glancing a round kick to her side, underneath her arm. He counted the point in his head, and spent the rest of the match playing keepaway, making sure she didn't score on him.

"*Geuman*!" Taemin called, when time ran out. They stood at attention again, and, panting, Marcus watched Taemin raise his arm in his direction. Match to him. He'd won two out of three.

They bowed to each other, and then Preeti spit out her mouth guard and dove at him for a hug. Marcus caught her, laughing.

"That was awesome!" she said, slapping the top of his helmet. "So much fun, we've got to do that more often."

Marcus grinned at her. It'd been a lot of fun. And Taemin beaming at them both, fairly dripping with pride, was nice too.

"Nice job," Mr. Avi said when they broke apart. "Both of you. That was pretty impressive, kid. Good job keeping up with her."

Marcus took out his mouth guard. "Thanks, Mr. Avi."

"That was so cool!" Jamal burst out. Roshen nodded enthusiastically. A few of the other adults came forward to talk about the match, and a couple of them asked if they could spar Marcus and

Preeti too. Marcus ended up doing rounds for almost the entire hour, in between breathing breaks and getting water.

"We're working you pretty hard," Taemin said, after Marcus finished a teaching match where he'd faced down Jamal and Roshen at the same time. "I hope you don't mind."

"Are you kidding? I'm having a great time."

"Good to hear! And I'm pretty impressed at how you're going. You clearly have been working on your stamina."

"Half of that's work on top of training," Marcus said. "Long days where I have to go for a long time over and over. It helps."

"I can tell." Taemin squeezed Marcus's shoulder. "It's a real pleasure to watch you."

Fuck that was good to hear. And it was just a compliment on his martial arts skill. He shouldn't be so *affected* by it. "Thanks," Marcus managed.

By the time Taemin led the class into a cooldown, Marcus felt loose, warm, and excited, in part because he was going to get Taemin to himself for the next while.

"You said you're going out with Master Choi now, right?" Preeti asked, as she and Marcus stowed their sparring equipment.

"Well, maybe not right now," Marcus said. "I think he'll probably want to do some of his own training before we leave."

Mr. Avi, who was next to them stowing his bo staff, gave Marcus a funny look. "Why would he do that? What do you think the last five hours were?"

"Uh, Taemin said that he normally trains by himself for an hour or two after classes were over on Saturday," Marcus said, confused.

Mr. Avi turned to point a finger at Taemin. "Master Choi!"

"What is it, Mr. Avi?" Taemin asked, coming over to them.

Mr. Avi glared at him. "I thought you said that since you'd started doing extra training on Sunday, you were making Saturday your rest day. Which still barely counts as a rest day, since you lead the whole conditioning class."

Taemin looked puzzled. "It is a rest day. Aside from the conditioning class, all I do is a little cardio work."

"That *counts*, sir," Mr. Avi growled. "You're going to run yourself into the ground."

Taemin rolled his eyes. "Honestly. I've been doing this since I was a child. I know perfectly well what I can handle."

"You sure about that? Did you even eat today?"

"Mr. Avi," Taemin said patiently, "I promise, as I have done several times, that I know how to look after myself."

"Did you?" Marcus asked.

"Did I what?"

"Eat today."

"Of course. I had breakfast before I came in to open the school."

Marcus frowned. "Nothing since then?"

Taemin looked bewildered. "I'm going out with you."

"You are?" Mr. Avi said.

Taemin nodded. "Marcus asked if we could get lunch together after class."

Mr. Avi looked between the two of them. "Okay," he said after a moment. "We won't keep you, then. Preeti and I can close up."

"That's all right," Taemin said. "I can—"

"Sir," Mr. Avi said, crossing his arms. "Preeti and I can handle it. Besides, look at it this way: you're keeping *Marcus* waiting."

"Oh," Taemin said, startled. "I—"

"It's okay," Marcus said quickly. "I don't want to upset your schedule." *Even if it might have needed to be interrupted.* Because Jesus Christ, Saturday was supposed to be his *rest* day? He was leading classes from eight to one and said he trained on his own for at least an hour or two after. And without breaks to eat? That was… that was pretty bad. No one could survive on that. And even if Taemin wasn't like this all the time, those were some bad habits. "But I wouldn't mind going sooner over later."

"Yes, yes, of course. I'm sorry. I didn't even think of that."

"Well now you can," Mr. Avi said. He made a shooing motion with his hand. "Preeti and I'll close up."

"Have a good time," Preeti said, waving at them.

Taemin looked at Marcus. "I guess I don't have a choice, do I?"

"Not really, sir."

Taemin swatted at him. "Stop that. Let me just get my things." Marcus followed him into the office, where Taemin grabbed up a duffel bag. "Do you mind if we make a pit stop at my apartment? If only to drop off my car. Though I really would like to grab a quick shower, if that's okay with you."

"Of course it is."

"All right." Taemin smiled brightly at him. "Meet you there?"

Marcus, for all that he was worried, couldn't help smiling back. "Yeah, okay."

IF TAEMIN was feeling a little bit shaky on the drive over to his apartment, he wasn't about to admit it to anyone. He had been feeling things a little harder lately, but then again, he also knew he was pushing himself harder too. In the years since his father had stepped down from running Choi's and transferred ownership squarely to Taemin, he'd only gained a workload. So on top of his regular training, volunteering, his work with the homeschool co-op, he was also responsible for an entire well-established school and five hundred students, give or take. It was very different from just working as an instructor, especially with what he had to live up to. And even with running the school itself, he still *was* an instructor. That part of being a Master was very important to him. He wasn't about to give up any of it.

But it did sometimes mean pushing himself harder and harder, as more things came up. And this year he was getting ready for the Olympic trials, too, which meant even more time spent training—and meeting with other high-ranks to keep himself in line. It was a lot of travel added to an already full schedule, and he'd been at it for several months. Would be at it for several more weeks, what with his qualifying tournament in June.

Preeti was forever stocking his office with snacks. He even had them once in a while, when he remembered. He should really try to remember more often. A protein bar or something around ten or eleven would probably have helped combat some of the fatigue he was feeling now.

Well, that was neither here nor there. Now he was going to spend time with Marcus, and he'd eat then. Plenty to look forward to. He wondered where Marcus might be interested in going. Taemin was sort of in the mood for a stir-fry dish of some sort. Carb and protein heavy, which was exactly what he'd need.

He parked and then went to the front of his building to wait for Marcus, who walked up to him a few minutes later. "Was the drive over too bad?"

"Nah," Marcus said with a smile. "GPS saves my life a lot."

Taemin laughed. "Same here. Well, come on in! I'm on the third floor." He led the way into the apartment's entry, and then went straight to the staircase before he faltered. "Sorry," he said. "The elevator's just down this way—"

Marcus put a hand on his shoulder. "I think I can manage the stairs," he said, voice colored with amusement.

Pleased, Taemin started up the three flights, then down the hall to his unit. "Here it is," he said, unlocking the door and showing Marcus inside.

Taemin quite liked his apartment. It was a two-bedroom, one bath, with an open living room/dining plan, a nice kitchen (which he really should use more often), and large windows that let in lots of natural light. He had it simply furnished, keeping much of the space open and airy, though plants were pretty much everywhere—a trait he'd gotten from his mother. The walls were mostly adorned with martial arts pieces: framed certificates that he didn't have up at Choi's; decorative mounts for his favorite weapons; a display made from the boards broken at his very first belt test, when he was a white belt barely three feet tall, and the boards from his first dan black belt test, and all of his old belts, in a ceremonial holder.

"Would you like something to drink?" he asked as he stepped out of his shoes.

Marcus shook his head. "I'm good. You said you wanted to take a shower?"

"If you don't mind. I can be quick."

"I don't mind at all. Go ahead." He gave Taemin a crooked grin. "I'll still be here when you get out. Might as well take the opportunity to change."

"Oh!" Of course Marcus had been working just as hard. Taemin was being a poor host, especially since Marcus had a change of clothes. "Would you like to shower too?"

Marcus looked startled. "Oh, uh—"

"If you want to," Taemin amended quickly. "Not that—not that there's any need. Just, I figured, you were working pretty hard. If you wanted to rinse off?"

Marcus huffed a laugh. "No offense taken. That'd be great. I'll hold off on changing, then, and just wait 'til you get out."

"I'll be out soon," Taemin assured him, before ducking into the bathroom.

He stripped down, leaving his clothes in a pile to scoop up and put in the laundry hamper once he was out of the shower, and stepped under the spray. It was a little odd to be taking a shower knowing Marcus was just in the next room. He didn't often have people over where that was something that'd take place.

Either way, since he was mostly soaping up to get the sweat off, he was finished quickly. Grabbed a towel for cursory dry-off so that he didn't keep Marcus waiting for his turn, then wrapped said towel around his waist and left the bathroom.

"Shower's yours," he said to Marcus, who was sitting on his couch and doing something with his phone.

Marcus looked up and dropped his phone. He swore and bent to pick it up, then stood, hefting his duffel. "Right! Yeah, thanks."

"Let me get you a towel." Taemin went to the linen closet and pulled out a fresh one, holding it out to Marcus.

Marcus took it in his free hand. "Thanks," he said, ducking his head. "I'll be out in a minute."

"No rush," Taemin assured him before turning to his bedroom.

He threw his sweat-soaked clothes in his laundry hamper, hung his towel up to be dealt with later, and then pulled on a pair of jeans and a black "Choi's Taekwondo Academy" T-shirt, which he had about a million of.

The door to the bathroom was still closed when he left his bedroom, so he swung by his kitchen to get a glass of water. He had to brace against his kitchen counter to deal with another wave of shakiness. Food. Food was probably a good idea.

"Everything okay?"

Taemin spun around to see Marcus watching him with an expression of concern. He was wearing cargo shorts and a fitted red V-neck, and droplets of water were escaping his curly hair and trailing down the side of his neck.

Taemin blinked hard. "Just fine," he said, putting the empty glass on the counter. "Ready?"

"Yeah," Marcus said after a moment. "Sure. Let's go."

Since they'd have to return to Taemin's place to drop him back off, Marcus left his duffel at the apartment, pulling his baseball cap low over his eyes again as they headed to his car. It was funny to think of him trying to use it as a disguise, as it did nothing to hide his well-angled face, the way his muscles moved under his shirt, his strong legs. Which was an odd thing to notice, Taemin felt. Though it wasn't as if it wasn't all true. Marcus was an attractive man. That was simply fact. The movie industry had even helped him build a career on it.

"What are you in mood for?" Marcus asked as they got inside his car.

"Do you not have a preference?"

Marcus shook his head. "I picked the last place we went to, remember?"

That was true. All right, then, Taemin did have a particular food he was craving. "Have you ever been to Little Tree? It's in Royal Oak. Specializing in Asian cuisine. It's got quite a good selection of food from different places, as well as sushi, if you like that."

Marcus's lips quirked as he started the car. "I live in California. I'd probably be excommunicated if I didn't like sushi. Little Tree it is." He set it on Google Maps, and away they went.

They drove in silence for a few minutes before Marcus said, "So you're training on Sundays too?"

Taemin nodded. "Of course. I need to make sure I'm in top form. Sunday is usually a good day for me to meet with other higher ranks, since most schools are closed then. I try to get together with someone every week for at least a few hours."

"But… didn't you do that Friday?"

"Well, yes. But again, I need to make sure I'm as good as I can be. And Sundays are still pretty restful. I train for two or three hours in the morning, and then I've got the rest of the day to myself." Granted, once he had started meeting with others to train, his days had gotten fuller recently, but—"Same with Saturdays really. Classes end at one. I do my own thing in the dojang for another hour or two, and then I've got the rest of the day."

"What do you tend to use your days off for?"

Taemin shrugged. "This and that. Errands mostly. Grocery shopping, laundry… the mundane stuff." He chuckled. "Though I'll admit, sometimes I wake up, work out, shower, eat, and then feel like going right back to bed."

"Yeah," Marcus said after a pause, "I can imagine."

"And you? How are you filling your days right now? When does filming start?"

"It's slated to start the Monday after next. Everyone else—the actors, rest of the crew, are all arriving tomorrow. Most of the sets are built, and what isn't yet will be done while we film other things. Next week's going to be filled with being walked through different areas, getting fitted for costumes, reuniting with the main cast and with Billy. I probably won't get my first day out of days until sometime later in the week."

"Day out of days?"

"It's a type of call sheet. It basically breaks down who is going to be doing filming when and where, for the week. They can change on a day-to-day basis sometimes, depending on a bunch of situations, so nothing's really set in stone, but it's nice to have. So for instance, it might say that me, Roger, and Hailey—she's the kid playing Roger's sister—are all supposed to be working on Tuesday. Or, if we're going to be doing scenes that Hailey isn't in, it might just call for me and Roger."

"That sounds like it can get complicated."

"You get used to it." Marcus laughed. "And it helps that I don't have to do anything but be where they tell me to be. And half the time I don't even need to get there myself; they send me cars. I'll tell you one thing I'm looking forward to, though."

"What's that?"

"The practice space. For all the fights and stunt work, we'll be working on blocking all throughout the filming process. We're renting space from Troy's Gymnastics, which is a huge open gym building. Because part of the movie takes place in space, we're doing a lot of zero-gravity action sequences, which sound like they'll be a lot of fun to work on."

"That does sound fun! I hope you enjoy it."

Marcus smiled at him. "Me too."

Chapter Five

MARCUS WASN'T ready to say goodbye once they finished eating. He was having a great time and it seemed like Taemin was too. Lunch had been lots of stories about their current lives interspersed with reminiscing, along with plenty of laughter. He hadn't felt this kind of connection to someone else in years.

"What do you have going on for the rest of the day?" he asked once he'd paid. Taemin had tried to protest, but Marcus had won in the end. "Any plans?"

Taemin shook his head. "Grocery shopping at some point. There's a store right by my apartment that I usually walk to. But if I go on a weekend, I usually go later in the day when less people tend to be there."

So Taemin had no real plans. "Well," Marcus said. "It's a nice day. And Royal Oak is a good meandering area. Want to go for a walk?"

"Sure." Taemin smiled.

They left the restaurant and set out, walking side by side down Main Street, drifting into easy, companionable silence. It was so nice to just be with someone and not feel like he had to entertain them.

Barely three days, and Marcus was pretty sure that he was in love. Hell.

"Marcus?"

"Sorry," Marcus said, coming back down to Earth. "Yeah?"

"Mind wandering?" Taemin asked, grinning cheekily at him.

You have no idea. "Maybe a little." He pinched his fingers together. "What did you say?"

Taemin pointed at a café right in front of them. "I was thinking about bubble tea. Did you want some?"

"Oh, uh, yeah. Sure."

"And I'll be paying this time," Taemin said, leveling him with a look.

Marcus held up his hands in surrender. "Okay, okay."

The café was pretty large, decorated in wood and wicker, with original art on the walls and a huge chalkboard displaying the menu.

"The bubble tea orders are over here," Taemin said to him, picking up two little laminated sheets and a dry-erase marker. "You select what you want to order here. It's very customizable."

"Hi, Taemin," the girl behind the counter said.

Taemin smiled at her. "Hi, Serena. How's the day going?"

"Pretty good." She glanced at the card in his hand. "Bubble tea today?"

Taemin nodded. "But it'll take a minute. I'll have my usual, but my friend hasn't been here before."

Serena smiled at Marcus. "Feel free to ask about our—" Her eyes widened. "No way."

Marcus hid a wince. Looks like he'd been recognized. Again, not unexpected, but it sort of interfered with the normalcy—and intimacy—of the time he had been having. "Hey," he said. "What's Taemin's regular? He comes here a lot, then?"

"Oh, uh, y-yeah." Serena looked between them. "Almond cocoa black milk tea, tapioca bubbles, no ice."

"I'm very set in my ways," Taemin put in. "Also, this way I don't have to decide what I'm going to order every single time."

"Sounds about right," Marcus said. He smiled at Serena and then made a show of looking at the little "flavor of the week" display. "Strawberry milk tea with the yogurt boba sounds interesting. I'll try that."

"Right! Yes, yeah, of course."

"And ring us up together please," Taemin said quickly, wallet already in hand.

Once she'd given Taemin the receipt, Serena went to make the bubble tea. It was only a few minutes before she was handing them over the counter to them.

"Um," she said, after giving Marcus his. "I-I hope you like it."

"Thanks." He waited.

"Could I have an autograph?" she burst out. "My sister and I love your movies."

Marcus glanced at Taemin, who was watching curiously, and smiled at Serena. "I'll do you one better. Want a selfie with me?"

"Oh my god, yes, please, Brooklyn will *die.*"

"That your sister?" Marcus asked as she came around the counter. She nodded. "Well, I appreciate you two being fans of mine."

A group of people had come into the café by the time Serena was done taking her pictures, and they were all looking curiously at Marcus. He recognized the mood of a crowd about to know who he was, so he quickly grabbed Taemin's elbow.

"Let's get back on that walk, huh?"

Taemin went easily, waiting until they were back on the street about half a block away before saying, "That must get tiresome."

Marcus knew what he was talking about, but he shook his head. Even if Taemin was right. "No, it's okay. Just comes as part of the package."

Taemin frowned. "Just because it's something you're used to doesn't mean it doesn't get old. It must. To be stopped all the time, or bothered, or stared at."

"Yeah," Marcus said after some hesitation. "Yeah it does, sometimes."

"I'm sorry about that."

"It's okay. Really. It's such a small thing, in the big picture."

"Well," Taemin said, voice light, "if you ever need a place where you know you won't be treated any differently, you have Choi's. Everyone's equal on the mat."

Marcus gave him a crooked smile and wished he could kiss him. "Thanks."

SUNDAY WAS Taemin's real day off. He trained and taught full-time Monday to Saturday, so Sunday was his day to rest and fully recharge. He often slept late (sometimes until *nine*), had an easy breakfast, and the rest of the day was for catching up on reading or other media (mostly training seminars and martial arts expos), lounging about his apartment, and actually using his kitchen. When asked, he normally would call Sundays "indulgence" days. Or they used to be.

Now, while his days didn't start at five like his Monday and Wednesday mornings, he was still up early to get ready for a full day of training. Even if he'd spent his whole life honing his skills, he always kicked it into high gear before a big competition—and the Olympic qualification tournament certainly counted for that. It was the start of May and the competition was the beginning of June, meaning he only had about a month left. He was confident in his abilities, but the worst thing he could do was rely on them and slack off in the last few weeks he had to better himself.

And maybe he was thinking too hard about the trials, but it would be his first, and probably only, attempt at the Olympics. Five years ago he had *just* begun to take on running Choi's. Traveling to compete in tournaments was the last thing on his mind. Now that he was more confident and more established as the current Master, with Preeti and Mr. Avi able to run classes without him if needed, he was able to do a little more for himself in the martial arts world. Not to mention that the more titles *he* had, the better his own reputation. It wouldn't do for the current Master of Choi's Taekwondo Academy—Ki-hyuk's American school and legacy—to seem as though he was stagnating. He'd been competing again in earnest for the last two years and doing quite well, if he did say so himself. Even with the embarrassment that had come from his little hiccup during nationals after he'd medaled.

He had a light breakfast—nothing too heavy before working himself hard—and then drove to the academy, already going over the day's planning in his head. Bodyweight strength-training, then an hour or two of static stretching, before moving on to speed and endurance drills. About four hours, give or take, with a few rest breaks in between. Then he'd go home to shower and eat, maybe fit in a nap, and drive down to Detroit, where he and two other Masters were meeting to train together and exchange techniques.

Once Taemin arrived at the dojang, he stowed his shoes and duffel bag, then went to change into his dobok. After he was dressed, he swung by his office to put on some music.

He stepped out into the empty mat, took a deep breath, and got started.

About two hours later, he was pulling himself out of his last stretch, perhaps stumbling just a little at the change from being on the floor to standing. Instead of reaching for his water bottle, he went into his office's minifridge to grab one of the bottles he kept in there. Filled with a cold mixture of lightly sweetened and salted green tea, a homemade drink his father swore by, it was a boost of energy from the sugar and an electrolyte renewal from the salt. He took a long pull, gasping a little when finished, then headed back out onto the mat to start his speed drills.

Taemin hadn't even gotten started when the bell over his door jingled. He turned to face the newcomer—probably a walk-in looking for information. He got those once in a while when he trained by himself, with the lights being on and the door being open.

His eyes widened in surprise to see Mr. Avi bowing into the building. He was wearing khakis and a polo, pretty typical weekend wear for him. Unless he was planning to change, he definitely wasn't looking to train.

"Hey," Mr. Avi said, eyeing him. "You're here. What a surprise."

"I'm probably more surprised than you are," Taemin said, coming over to him. "What are you doing here?"

Mr. Avi crossed his arms. "I'm here to talk some sense into you. I know for a fact you're going to be training yourself into the ground this afternoon. Which means that you should be taking it easy *now.* And you're not. Can't say I'm shocked."

"Mr. Avi—"

"And I showed up because I knew I had a better chance of talking you out of it in person. Julia is waiting for me to report back."

"You and Julia worry too much," Taemin said, exasperated. "I'm doing fine."

Mr. Avi glared. "If Marcus hadn't clued me in to your plans yesterday, you would have been on the mat for seven hours. That's too much!"

"My last black belt test lasted for twelve," Taemin pointed out.

"Yeah, and you have those how often, exactly?"

That was a point. And Taemin knew he'd been working hard. But still. "I'm already here and warmed up. I should do one hour of cardio at least." Mr. Avi did not stop glaring. "And then I'll stop. I promise."

"Until your meeting at three?"

"It's only ten," Taemin said stubbornly. "That's plenty of time to rest."

"Well if you're going to go for another hour, you're at least eating something," Mr. Avi said in a voice that brooked no argument. He headed into Taemin's office. Taemin followed him, at a bit of a loss.

While Mr. Avi rummaged through the boxes of nonperishables that he and Preeti had left—and wow, Taemin hadn't realized how much he'd acquired, considering he had stopped paying attention after a while—Taemin figured he might as well check his phone. He was pleased to find he had a message from Marcus.

Hey, hope you're having a good morning so far. It's my last day before work really starts for me, so I was wondering if you wanted to maybe get coffee or something together? Totally cool if you can't, I know you're training today, but just thought I'd ask. Even if we don't get together today, hopefully we can again this week? If only to maybe spend some time together on the mat. Let me know!

"Good news?" Mr. Avi asked, holding out a package of trail mix.

Taemin realized he was smiling at his phone. He set it down to take the trail mix and tear open the package. "Marcus. He was wondering if we couldn't meet again today." That'd be nice. Maybe a break before he went to Detroit was warranted after all.

"You should. Give yourself a break." When Taemin nodded, mouth full of trail mix, Mr. Avi asked, "When did he come into town anyway?"

"Hm?" He swallowed. "I'm not sure. But he came here Wednesday night, and we talked some before he invited me out for breakfast on Thursday. We got together before that, to spar a little."

"Okay," Mr. Avi said slowly. "And then he came to the dojang Thursday after class. And then Saturday for class."

Taemin ate some more trail mix. "Mm-hm."

"And you two went out after class on Saturday, right?"

"Right."

"And he's inviting you out again now."

Taemin finished the trail mix and threw the bag in the trash. "I'm really enjoying getting to spend so much time with him. And he's being very nice, to keep inviting me out." Especially with how much Marcus seemed to have going on in his life. After all, his last free day before launching into a huge project like being in a movie? And he was making time to spend with Taemin? That was a total pleasure.

"Uh-huh." Mr. Avi handed him a protein bar, which Taemin took without protest. "Well, okay. That counts as a break in my book, as long as he's not asking to meet you for, I don't know, an afternoon of parkour."

Taemin rolled his eyes while he chewed. "He said coffee," once he'd swallowed.

Mr. Avi leveled him with an unreadable expression, before he shrugged and slapped Taemin on the shoulder. "Sounds good to me. If you like seeing him, you should take him up on it."

Taemin smiled back down at his phone. "I think I will."

MONDAY FOUND Marcus awake bright and early in order to get his workout in before meeting with Billy in a Panera for an in-person get-together to talk over what would be going on for the week. After he'd given Marcus a tentative schedule (and pointed out everything in the Google calendar they shared), they'd head over to the gymnastics place to meet the director, producer, and stunt coordinator, along with some of the other main cast, to start getting run-downs and blocking. The next week would mostly be long days at the gym, interspersed with getting new versions of the script to look over, costume fittings, and makeup tests; his character design called for a pretty intricate back tattoo, which was supposed to be part of a big reveal in the plot later on in the movie.

He finished his workout, jumped in and out of the shower, pulled on a T-shirt and pair of shorts, then checked his phone to let Billy know he was on his way.

Aside from a text from Billy (and an email with the latest version of the script to look over later), he also had one from Taemin. *Wishing you good luck on your first day at work!*

Warmth bloomed inside Marcus, knowing that Taemin was thinking about him. *Thanks*, he typed back. *I hope you have a great day.* He stowed his phone in his pocket, grabbed his wallet and keys, and left the apartment.

"So," Billy asked after he and Marcus took a seat in a little tucked-away corner booth. "Are you settled in yet?"

"Probably more than you are," Marcus said. He'd been in Michigan for almost a week now. Billy'd arrived last night. "How was the flight in?"

Billy groaned. "Miserable, considering the time difference, but isn't it always?"

"Hey, better than when we had to go to Australia."

He sighed. "True. Now then." He set a binder and a tablet on the table. "Let's talk shop, shall we?"

Two hours later and they'd covered Marcus's tentative schedule for the whole week. When he was going to costuming (tomorrow morning), when he was getting his first sit-down with the other main characters in the cast (Wednesday afternoon, though he'd be seeing a lot of them today and tomorrow anyway, as they all were in and out of wardrobe and the gym), and so on.

"I think that about covers it," Billy said, after he'd made sure the last appointment he had with Marcus for that week had synced to both their phones' calendars.

"As always, I'm a grateful man."

"Oh, don't worry," Billy said with a grin, "I'm very aware of how important I am."

Marcus laughed. "Meet you at the gym?"

Billy nodded. "Please don't get lost and end up in Canada."

"Excuse you, I have never crossed state borders getting lost."

"And let's keep it that way, shall we?"

Billy's ribbing aside, Marcus did make judicious use of Google Maps in order to get to the gymnasium where he was supposed to meet everyone else. He made good time, though, pulling up just as Billy was getting out of his own car.

"See?" he called. "Made it!" Even from the distance, he could see Billy roll his eyes.

They walked to the building together, following the signs that pointed them to where they needed to be. It was pretty obvious they were in the right place when he saw a few guys he recognized.

"Leo! Hey man, how you been?"

Leo Gonzales, a mountain of a man and one of the best damn stunt coordinators Marcus had ever had the pleasure of working with, came over to greet them. "Marcus!" He took Marcus's outstretched hand and pulled him in for a hug, slapping him on the back. "Good to be working with you again." Beaming, he turned to Billy. "Hey Billy. It's—it's nice to see you."

"Leo," Billy said, voice bland.

Leo's smile faltered. "Uh, yeah." He cleared his throat. "Anyway, let's have you say hi to everyone else, huh?"

TAEMIN GOT home Monday after class at around ten o'clock and immediately dropped his things to head straight for the shower. Even though he'd managed to squeeze in a nap that afternoon, getting up at five to lead the early-morning sparring class and then not being done at work until the evening adult class was over at eight thirty.... He had left attendances to go over tomorrow morning, instead heading home as soon as he and Preeti said goodbye.

Once he was clean and dressed to sleep in soft lounge pants and a worn T-shirt, he went into the kitchen to grab something to eat. While he ate, he absentmindedly checked his phone for the first time in hours. A few emails relating to the school, another one from his mother asking how he was doing, the usual text from Preeti to let him know she'd gotten home safe (something he insisted she send him every evening), and a text from Marcus, sent around 8:00 p.m.

Just got done with a long day. Though I shouldn't complain, since I know for a fact that yours was even longer than mine. Even so, I hope it was a good day for you.

The emails Taemin figured could wait until he was more awake, but he typed out a reply to Marcus. Even if he was asleep now, he could wake up to the message.

It's true my day was long, but it was a good one. I hope your day was the same.

Surprisingly, he received a reply almost immediately. *It was, thanks. Got a lot done. And it was nice to see some of the crew again.*

Good to hear, Taemin sent back. *Is tomorrow another full day?* Today had to have been, if Marcus had only gotten home a few hours ago.

Probably not quite as long as this one, since we had to cram a lot in, what with everyone only just getting here. Tomorrow will be meeting with costumes and makeup. Wednesday is when we start cast reads, and we're slated to start filming the easier stuff next week.

Already? Wow! That's pretty soon. Does all movie making go that fast?

Yes and no, Marcus wrote. *A lot of it really boils down to hurry up and wait. We all rush to be somewhere and then have to wait ages for setup, or timing is imperative and then a take needs to be redone twenty times. We've already got the infinity room set up, so we'll be filming there for a while, before we head downtown to do the on-set stuff.*

That's really interesting. If you're ever up for it, I'd love to hear more about the process and how things are going for you. He finished eating and got up to clear everything away. His phone buzzed several times before he grabbed it again, taking it with him as he went into his bedroom.

That'd be great, Marcus had written. *I'd love to see you again. What is your week looking like?*

Taemin sighed. *Pretty busy. But then again, it always is. I have pockets of free time during the day, but I'm sure you'd be busy then. And I can't ask to see you at night during or after classes, after you've had a long day.*

There wasn't a swift reply this time, so Taemin assumed that Marcus had gone to bed. It wasn't a bad idea for him to do so either. He set his phone down on his nightstand and crawled under his covers. Just as he was about to turn off his bedside lamp, his phone lit up again.

Long day or not, I'd like to see you. Even if it's just for a little while. I'd really like to come by after class tomorrow. If you didn't mind.

Of course I don't mind. But classes end at 8:30. Are you sure you want to be out that late?

If it means seeing you, then yeah.

Taemin blinked down at his phone, the rush of warmth at reading those words startling in its ferocity. He was tired. He was overthinking what Marcus probably meant.

What Taemin had just realized he maybe wanted it to mean, after the time they'd been spending together recently.

No, he was being ridiculous. And possibly overstepping by even thinking Marcus might be interested in anything more than platonic. Marcus had been his *student.* As a child no less. Taemin was upset at himself for even entertaining the idea. That there might be something more there.

But… what was the best course of action here? Now that he knew he was interested in Marcus—and how couldn't he be, seeing the kind, strong, attractive man he'd grown up into—would it be… right to keep spending time with him? So much time?

Then again, it wasn't as if Taemin was the one asking Marcus out. It had been Marcus who had continued to ask if they could meet, in part because Taemin didn't want to push too hard in trying to reconnect, if Marcus didn't want to.

But… it seemed that Marcus did want to. At least in some respect.

"Stupid," Taemin muttered, frowning down at his phone. He was tired and overthinking things, was all. And now he'd kept Marcus waiting while he dithered. *I'm always happy to see you*, he ended up sending, trying for innocuous but truthful. *Talk to you more later? I'm turning in.*

Good night, Marcus sent back. *Sleep well.*

Chapter Six

MARCUS ALWAYS kinda liked costuming. It was cool to see what artists and designers came up with considering guidelines they might or might not have been given. And he was lucky in that he didn't mind trying on and changing clothes.

His measurements had been taken before he'd left of course, so when he showed up for fittings, it was to dozens and dozens of options, all in varying degrees of interesting and raggedy, to try on and model for the director to see what worked and what didn't. There wouldn't be a whole lot of costume changes in the film, what with his character being a space-rat, so it was important to find the right look. It would essentially help sell the film, since he was the main promoter of it.

He didn't even know how long it'd been when he came out of the dressing room in yet another mix-n-match jumble of pieces and it was decided they'd found what they were looking for: Dark-wash jeans (space always managed to have jeans) with artfully splattered drops of paint, oil, and grease stains, a dark red shirt flecked with gray, and a black bomber jacket. Steel-toed work boots and fingerless gloves completed the look. Not that interesting, to be honest. Way tamer than some of the initial pieces they'd had him try on. "What do you think?" he asked Billy as he was posed for pictures to document the chosen costume.

Billy didn't even look up from his phone. "You just spent over an hour trying stuff on to get that look. You think I'm going to say anything that isn't positive?"

Marcus snorted. "Come on."

Billy glanced at him. "You look fine. Very space-dystopia leading-man material."

"Thanks."

"What do you want to do for lunch, by the way? I know we've got some time—" Marcus hadn't even gotten to makeup yet. "—but better if I know sooner over later."

Marcus gave Billy a funny look. "I'm meeting with Leo and the guys for lunch, remember?" He knew he'd be seeing them a lot soon—probably to the point that they'd all be sick of each other (although always in a friendly way), but he was sort of eager to talk shop.

"Oh." Billy dropped his gaze right back down to his phone. "Right. Sorry, I forgot."

"No worries," Marcus said quickly. Billy prided himself on his professionalism, no matter the close relationship he and Marcus had. He'd be kicking himself for forgetting something even as simple as what Marcus was doing for lunch off the clock. "I think I only mentioned it in, like, passing anyway. Probably didn't give you a lot of notice to write it down."

"Will you need me at lunch, then?"

Marcus shook his head. "Nah. You can go do your own thing after we're done here." Since everyone was doing wardrobe stuff today, he didn't need to be at the gym until tomorrow, after he met with London, Roger, and Hailey (and Hailey's mom) to discuss the script.

Billy nodded, looking relieved. "Okay. Easy enough."

Once he was given the go-ahead, Marcus went to change back into his street clothes—consisting of shorts again, since it was so nice out. It was going to be murder to film outside in his chosen costume once it started getting really hot. Just something to look forward to. Then he and Billy walked down the hallway to makeup.

He immediately had to take off his shirt again, in order for tests to start on his back tattoo. Gone were the days of Marcus not appreciating the work that went into altering a character's appearance in any way, shape, or form. Makeup artists were gods, possessing knowledge of intricate witchcraft, and they were to be feared. Lest they utilize the same patience and insanity that allowed them to hand-letter tiny script tattoos over an entire person's body and use it for evil.

It did, however, also leave him with a lot of time just sitting backward in a chair.

"Pink script is out," Billy told him, handing Marcus his phone. "If you wanted to read through that while you wait."

"Thanks." Marcus unlocked his phone but, instead of going to his email, went to his messages instead.

So what are the odds that the movie industry will take me as a martial artist stunt double in the event med school kills me? Preeti had sent, along with a picture of three textbooks and an open laptop.

Not that high, considering you'd be dead, Marcus sent back, amused. *But if you're interested in actually doing stunt work, I can pass along your info to my stunt coordinator.*

Oh my GOD no thank you times a billion.

Marcus's amusement skyrocketed. *Not a fan of being in front of the camera?*

Nope nope nope.

What about the eventual speeches you'll be giving when you become the best sports medicine doctor in the world?

Shadow puppets.

Marcus chuckled. *Still means you need to survive medical school.*

Yeah, yeah. Are you coming by the dojang anytime this week? I can get some of my energy out.

I was going to see if I couldn't stop by tonight. Make the adult class. Will you be there?

Yeah! I work Tuesday nights.

Cool. I'll see you tonight then.

Awesome, yeah.

He went from messages to email then, to pull up the pink script and start reading through it, but he only got a few paragraphs in before he got another message. From Taemin this time. Eagerly, he went to read it.

Preeti just told me you're going to be a guest at class tonight again. She used a lot of exclamation marks, so I think she might be excited about it.

As long as you're okay with it, Marcus wrote back. *I know I've sort of been taking over the dojang a little bit.*

Stop that. I told you I'm happy to have you. I meant it then, I mean it now.

Marcus couldn't help his smile. *You're going to be seeing a lot more of me, then.*

As long as you don't push yourself too hard!

Hey, right back atcha. How's the day been treating you? This was a volunteer day for you, right?

Right. And it was… it was all right. I awarded a black belt today. That's always hard.

Marcus had to swallow. A black belt award ceremony at Kids Kicking Cancer was done near the end of a child's life. *I'm so sorry.*

The response took almost a full minute of ellipses appearing and disappearing before he got a simple: *Her name is Lila. I've been seeing her since January.*

And then

I'm going to miss her so much.

Are you going to be okay? Marcus asked, feeling like it wasn't enough.

I'll be fine, thank you.

Marcus bit his lip, then typed, *What else do you have to do today?*

Nothing until class starts at 4:30 pm. I'll probably just go to the academy anyway though. Work my body a little.

One way to mourn. But…. *Do you want some company? I've got a couple hours free coming up.* Leo and the guys would understand if he skipped out on lunch. Besides, they'd have plenty of time to see each other in the coming months.

It's okay. You don't have to do that.

I want to, Marcus quickly replied. *If company would help.*

Are you sure?

Yeah, absolutely. Just tell me where to be, and I'll let you know when I'm on my way over.

Maybe I'll go home then. For a little while.

Sure, yeah. Maybe try to take a nap?

That's a good idea. Okay.

And I'll see you in an hour or two, all right? Do you want me to just meet you at your apartment?

That would be nice. Thank you.

Of course, Marcus wrote. *I'll see you soon.*

He sighed heavily, went to text Leo to let him know he wouldn't be making it, and then lifted his head to see Billy watching him curiously. "What's up?"

"Nothing," Billy said after a second. "You okay, though? You look kind of upset. Bad news?"

Marcus rubbed at his face. "You could say that."

"What's wrong?"

Marcus swallowed again. "Taemin basically just had a student die."

Billy's eyes widened. "What?" And then, "Wait, who's Taemin?"

Marcus shrugged (followed by an apology to the makeup artists). "Taemin was my old teacher, remember?"

"You mean… Master Choi? That guy you always talk about?"

"Uh, yeah."

Billy nodded seriously. "And what happened?"

Marcus explained about Taemin's volunteer work, and what today meant to him. When he was done, Billy looked heartbroken. "Wow," he said. "That's…."

"Yeah. Yeah, it's heavy. So I just… I want to be there for him, you know?"

"Yeah, of course," Billy said quickly. "Although, uh, so we're clear, this *is* the guy you've basically been in love with for all time, right?"

"Not *all* time," Marcus mumbled.

"Semantics."

"Then yeah. Kind of."

"Got it. Okay. Then what's the plan of action?"

"What do you mean?"

"He's upset. You care about him. What are you going to do?"

"Oh uh—" Marcus fumbled, taken aback by how onboard Billy was. "I was going to keep him company after I got done with makeup."

"That's a good idea. Did you want me to let Leo know you won't be meeting him?"

"Already did it," Marcus said, holding up his phone. "I figure I'll just take a Lyft to his place and then back to my apartment." Billy had picked him up to take him to costuming that day.

"Okay. Okay, good." Billy fidgeted with the hem of his shirt. "I hope you guys are able to figure things out, by the way. You deserve the best."

Marcus had to smile. "Thanks, Billy."

"And he must be incredible, considering how gone on him you are. You've got pretty high standards."

Or they were high in the first place because no one ever managed to match up to Marcus's ideal. Which was utterly ridiculous if one thought about it: a kid being in love with his mentor, only to reunite with him later and not only realize that, yes, he still was totally absolutely in love, but that said mentor was even *more* of an amazing human being than originally observed. What the hell. Marcus was either going to be the luckiest man alive or a sorry bastard, depending on how things worked out.

"He is," Marcus sighed. "He really is."

TAEMIN WASN'T hungry when he got home, too heartbroken over the events of the day to think about eating. He stepped out of his shoes and made a beeline for his bedroom, crawling under the covers and cocooning himself, trying to—not forget, he'd never want to forget Lila—but to find some peace.

He did end up falling into an exhausted sleep, but it was fitful, tossing and turning as he drifted in and out of consciousness. His phone buzzing on the nightstand was a welcome distraction, even as he blinked awake to see that it was from Marcus, letting him know that he was finished with work for the day and that he was heading over.

Taemin set his phone back down on his nightstand and sat up, rubbing at his face. He was probably being selfish, accepting Marcus's offer. Marcus was taking so much time for him.

But Taemin hadn't wanted to be alone. And Marcus… they'd only spent a few days together so far, so Taemin had no idea how his presence had become such a comfort, but it had. So quickly that it was a little frightening. He knew he should be trying to give Marcus some distance. Still, he'd… he'd take comfort where he could get it right now. He didn't want to begrudge himself that.

He swung his legs out of bed and stood, tucking his phone into his pocket on the way to the bathroom, where he washed his face to remove the sleep grit. It was also probably time to eat something, and it was easy enough to pull out some leftover pasta and warm it up while he sipped on some water.

When he finished eating, he washed the dishes to give himself something to do, then aimlessly wandered into his living room. He ended up folding himself down onto his couch to try to meditate while he waited for Marcus.

The buzzer blaring out in his apartment jerked him back to reality, and he hurried to buzz Marcus inside, not bothering to do anything but wait in his foyer, shifting from foot to foot. He yanked open his door as soon as he heard the first knock, a startled expression flashing across Marcus's face before it collapsed into concern. "Hey," he said quietly.

"Hello," Taemin replied, just as quiet, stepping back to allow Marcus inside. "Thank you for coming."

"Of course. I—whatever you need." Marcus toed out of his shoes, closed the door behind him.

"Do you want something to drink?"

Marcus shook his head. "I'm fine. Do you… do you maybe want to sit down?"

Taemin followed listlessly as Marcus steered him toward his couch, sitting when Marcus sat, hands coming up to clasp together.

"Taemin?"

"Yes?"

"Do you mind if I touched you right now? Is that okay?"

Taemin swallowed. "That'd be okay." More than okay. He really could do with a hug.

Marcus put an arm around Taemin's shoulders and pulled him closer, Taemin going easily until he was pressed up against Marcus's side, head resting on his chest. Taemin turned in toward him, and Marcus brought up both his arms, enveloping him. Just… just holding him.

"I'm so sorry," Marcus murmured.

Taemin nodded, words gone, and just held on tight.

MARCUS WASN'T sure how long they sat there together in silence, just breathing with each other, Taemin a warm weight against him. He hoped he was being a comfort. That was all he wanted to be right now: a comfort and a support. And he wasn't going to move until Taemin did.

Eventually Taemin did pull back, though, scrubbing at his eyes. "Thank you," he mumbled. "I'm sorry I—I'm sorry."

"You've got nothing to apologize for," Marcus rushed to say. "I'm happy I could be here, if you needed me."

Taemin looked at him then, so long and hard that Marcus started to sweat. Had he overstepped? Gone too far? Fuck, he might've—and especially now, with Taemin tired and sad and vulnerable, that was the worst thing he could have done.

But then Taemin just nodded. "Thank you," he said again. "I—I did. Need you, I think."

"Of course," Marcus managed. "Of course."

Taemin cleared his throat and then stood up completely. “Are you sure you don’t want something to drink?”

The change in subject was obvious, but Marcus latched on to it. Anything else he wanted to do, to say, needed to wait for a better moment anyway. “Some water would be good.”

“All right. I’ll be right back.” Taemin went to the kitchen and Marcus stayed on the couch, giving him some distance.

He returned shortly with two glasses, handed one to Marcus, and then sat right back down on the couch, but a short distance away this time.

It felt like miles.

“I’ve got an idea,” Marcus said, trying for light. “If you maybe wanted another distraction?”

“Yes?”

“Well, uh, you said you haven’t seen any of my movies. Were you maybe interested in watching one? I promise to pick a good one.”

“Oh. I….” Taemin considered it. “I think I’d like that. Sure.”

“Awesome. If you’ve got cable or, or want to let me sign into Netflix or something, I can pull one up easy.” He coughed. “Not to, uh, not to brag. They’re just, you know, kind of popular.”

At that, Taemin finally smiled. Small, but real. “I’m sure you deserve it. I have satellite, and that comes with pay-per-view.” He mostly used it to watch matches and documentaries.

“Well, that’s easy, then. The one I had in mind would be on pay-per-view.”

“Okay, sure.”

Marcus smiled and pulled up *All In*, a James Bond-type film with some of his best fight scenes. It was also one of his first movies with a male love interest, which he thought Taemin might appreciate.

By the time they were halfway through the movie, Taemin looked a little more invested in the plot and a little less distraught, which Marcus counted as a huge win. At Taemin’s insistence and questions, he also kept up a bit of a running commentary of how things were made and his thoughts and experiences during filming.

"I liked that a lot," Taemin said, once the credits started to roll. "You're very good. Though it's a little weird to see you be… not you."

Marcus laughed. "I get that. It's a little weird for me, too, to be honest. I've always got to separate myself from myself when I'm working, if that makes sense."

Taemin nodded. "I understand. You have different personas, depending on the situation. I think we're all like that, in some way. For instance, I've had some people tell me they find me intimidating. Me!"

Marcus wiggled a hand. "Well, I mean… I can see that."

"What? Really?"

He shrugged. "Well, you're very focused. Know what you want. Command a certain amount of respect. It makes sense to me. Only if someone didn't know you, though."

Taemin pursed his lips. "I'm not sure how I feel about that. I hope to be approachable, you know? My style might be traditional, but I don't exactly go around whacking people with sticks."

"No, you just make them sink into horse-stance and balance the stick on their knees."

"It builds character," Taemin insisted, finally, finally sounding completely like himself again. "And works on proper form. That's important."

Marcus held up his hands in surrender. "I wasn't disagreeing with you."

"Yes. Well. Good."

Marcus checked his watch. Three forty-five. "It's a quarter to four," he said. "In case you wanted to get ready for the academy." Part of him wanted to keep Taemin in the apartment, but the rest of him knew Taemin would do well to get on the mat for a while and put the rest of the day's events out of his mind.

Predictably, Taemin got to his feet. "Thank you for letting me know," he said. "I usually get there around four to make sure we're open for anyone showing up early. And that's when Preeti gets there on Tuesdays usually too. Though she has her own key now."

Huh. Preeti had a key to the building and was clearly able—and trusted—to run classes on her own. That was good to know. "Does she or Mr. Avi ever run the school when you're not there?"

"Hm? Oh yes, once in a while. If I have to travel for a tournament or to meet with other people in the circuit. I try not to be away too often, but the last few months have been busier than usual."

"Getting ready for the trials?" Marcus asked. Taemin had told him about the Olympic elimination tournament. He was understandably impressed.

"Right."

"Gotcha. Okay. Well, uh, I think I'm going to head out for now. Maybe swing by later tonight"—*to see how you're doing*—"but for now I'll get out of your hair."

"Marcus—"

"Yeah?"

Taemin looked up at him, then dropped his gaze to the floor. "Thank you," he said quietly. "For everything. It means a lot to me."

Marcus had to swallow. Had to stop himself from taking that extra step forward to gather him up in his arms again. He would say something. He would. But not today. "Of course. Anytime. And I—I mean that."

Taemin's eyes went wide and startled, so Marcus hurried to say his goodbyes before he could say too much more.

Chapter Seven

PREETI WAS already at the academy when Taemin arrived, stretching on the mat. She bounced to her feet to bow to him when he came in, and then dropped right back into the splits. "Hi, sir," she said.

Taemin put his shoes in a cubby. "Afternoon. How was school today?"

Preeti groaned. "I am looking forward to finals, if only so I'll be done with this semester. Of course, then that means *next* semester starts, but… one thing at a time, right?"

"Right."

"But hey." She grinned. "Marcus said he'd name-drop me if I ever wanted to be in a movie. Not that I would ever, ever let that happen, but the thought is nice. If I'm desperate."

Marcus. Taemin tried to smile and share Preeti's joke. "That was nice of him."

"Yeah. He really is! Nice, I mean. I'm liking getting to know him again, now that we're both older. And it's cool to see how being famous didn't, you know, change him much."

"It shows he has good character," Taemin said, almost automatically.

"Yeah. Not everyone would be like that." She moved into a different stretch. "I'm looking forward to him coming by again tonight. Maybe he'll take us out for dinner again."

"Don't try taking advantage of him," Taemin scolded. Because considering what Marcus had done so far, he probably *would* let Preeti talk him into dinner again. Although, now that he thought of it…. "When he said he was coming over, did he offer, or did you ask him to?"

"Huh?" Preeti glanced up at him. "Um, I think I asked if he wanted to spar again? And he said he was planning to swing by."

Ah. Preeti had broached the subject. Taemin wondered if Marcus had even thought about saying no. He had to be busy, had to be tired—Taemin already felt bad that Marcus had taken time out of his day to… be there for him. Now he was planning on coming by yet again. Maybe Taemin should talk to him. Tell him it wasn't expected, no matter how much Taemin enjoyed seeing him.

For now, though, he went to change, and by the time he was finished, his first group of students were arriving for his kid's class. He made small talk with parents, greeted children, and generally settled into being Master Choi for the next several hours.

Marcus still managed to worm his way into his thoughts, though, especially once Jamal and Roshen showed up for the adult class. Marcus had been so good with them, taking their admiration in stride and then using it to focus their energy, coaching them on how to spar. He'd made a good teacher. He'd only been back in Taemin's life for a week but it felt like he *fit.*

And it was… it was so wonderful, having him be a part of Taemin's life, in the capacity he was now. He hoped he would continue to be, now that they'd reconnected. A friend to talk to, to spend time with. A dear friend.

Taemin had no business wanting anything more.

"All right," he said when there was about twenty minutes left of class, "sparring gear on!"

"Sir!" The class at large scurried over to their bags to put on their gear. Preeti brought over his helmet for when he participated in matches. Taemin didn't bother putting on the whole set of pads for what was, for him, essentially play time. He mostly presided or participated in teaching spars on weeknights. Monday and Wednesday early-morning class and Saturdays were when he geared up at the academy.

"I wonder why Marcus isn't here yet." Preeti looked disappointed. "He said he would be."

"Something probably just came up," Taemin said. Trying not to worry. Marcus didn't seem like the type to say he would be somewhere and then not show.

As if on cue, the bell rang over the door as Marcus bowed into the building. He was wearing his street clothes, and he waved to them, expression rueful, then pointed to the office after taking off his shoes.

Taemin nodded, and Marcus smiled before heading into it.

Taemin and Preeti exchanged a confused glance. Taemin went to bow off the mat and go into the office himself.

"Hey," Marcus said in a rush. "Sorry I'm late. I didn't want to make, like, a scene and interrupt the class, so I figured I'd just hide in here for a little bit."

Taemin peered out of the office. Jamal and Roshen had gone over to Preeti, looking eager. Preeti made an unimpressed face and shrugged. Taemin turned back to Marcus. "You're free to stay in here if you want to avoid your fan club. But you also didn't have to come by, if it was going to be a bother for you."

Marcus shook his head. "It's not. At all. I wanted to. I just ended up going out to dinner with some people from set, and it ran late. I wanted to be here."

He kept saying that. But it had just been established that Marcus was simply that kind of person, who was kind and genuine and gave things his all. Taemin tried to smile. "You're always welcome."

Marcus blinked at him. "Are—what's the matter?"

"What? Nothing."

"I—okay. If you say so."

Taemin cleared his throat. "I'll send Preeti in to say hi, if you'd like? I know she was looking forward to seeing you tonight."

"Oh, uh, sure. If you don't mind."

"Of course. Give me a minute."

"HEY," PREETI said, coming into Taemin's office. She was in full sparring gear, minus her mouth guard. "Looks like you aren't up for sparring tonight, huh?"

"Sorry," Marcus said. "I was out later than I thought. I didn't have time to grab any workout wear."

She nodded. "It's okay. But you know, you didn't have to, like, come by. I know you've got stuff to do. You could've just sent an apology text. I would've gotten it after class."

"Yeah, I know. I wanted to, though."

"So you could… sit here in Master Choi's office?"

Marcus shrugged, unsure of what to say. That he wanted to check on Taemin because he'd been worried? That he wanted to see him anyway, regardless? That the academy felt like home and that Marcus wanted to be a part of the life of the man who ran it?

He waved an idle hand. "I just wanted to see him. And you, of course."

She tilted her head, expression calculating. Marcus was good at expressions. "Of course. Well. I'm getting back out there. Since *someone* decided to not show up ready to challenge me, I'm going to have to get some semblance of a workout from my students."

Marcus saluted her. "Have fun."

She saluted back and then left, her ponytail swinging behind her.

Alone in the office now, Marcus sat back and took a good long look around. There were certain things he recognized, like certificates and awards, and some things he didn't—mostly pictures of students. There was a whole wall nearly papered in pictures of kids and adults alike holding up medals or trophies or wearing new belt colors with old ones hanging around their necks, Taemin in all of them, standing to the side and looking proud.

As he followed the line of photos, they got older and older looking, and Taemin started looking younger. Then he came across one that made his breath catch.

It was him. At thirteen, wearing his junior black belt, holding his old bodan belt in his hands. A twenty-two-year-old Taemin had his arm slung around his shoulders, and they were both grinning at the camera. After all these years, after all the students who undoubtedly had to have come and gone… Marcus was still up there.

Marcus reached a hand out as if to touch, then pulled it back, his emotions in turmoil. Was he—was he right in wanting to pursue Taemin? After all this time? When they'd started out as student and teacher? Or would he alienate him by even suggesting it?

He didn't know how long he'd stared at the picture when his phone beeped with a message from Billy: *Schedule update, the cast read was moved to nine. Please confirm.*

Got it, Marcus sent back. His phone beeped again almost immediately.

How are things? Did you go back to the school like you planned to?

Yeah, Marcus wrote, *I'm here now. Went over after I was done with dinner.*

Okay? If you're texting me, you're there but you're not with him. What's going on?

Nothing, Marcus sent back, feeling bitter. *Just reevaluating my life choices.*

His phone rang. Billy. Marcus glanced out of the office to see that class was still going strong, and answered. "Yeah?" he said quietly.

"Reevaluating *what*?" Billy demanded. "You've been in love with this guy since you were a kid."

"Exactly," Marcus said in a furious whisper. "Since I was a kid. *He* saw me as a kid."

"But you're not one *now*."

"I know that. I know that, but I—I don't want to ruin a good thing. Being around him is enough. It's enough."

"For chrissakes, of course it isn't. You're pining. You don't pine. You are *in love*. It's not worth it to see where things could go?"

"And if I mess it up? You of all people should—" He cut himself off; that was *not* something he had the right to bring up, especially not now. "—I don't want to ruin it," he ended up repeating. "I don't want to lose what I have now."

Billy blew out an angry breath. Marcus could picture him raking a hand through his hair. "Fuck, just—fine. Fine. Don't tell him. But I want to say one more thing."

"Yeah?"

"If this guy really is as special as you think he is, even if he had to turn you down, I don't think he'd want you out of his life. That's—that's worth keeping in mind."

Marcus turned to look back at the picture. That Taemin had kept up, all these years. "Yeah. Yeah, it is."

AFTER CLASS had been dismissed and the last of the stragglers had left, Taemin and Preeti both went to change into street clothes and then met back in Taemin's office. Marcus looked up from his phone when they both came in.

"Hey," he said, offering up a smile. "Thanks for letting me stick around."

Preeti raised an eyebrow. "Because it was so much trouble, you holing up in here?"

Marcus shrugged. "Still. I'm here in your space, and it wasn't as if I was doing anything productive."

Taemin frowned. "Please don't think like that. You don't need to be doing something here. I'm happy to have you just be in the office."

At that, Marcus's lips quirked up. "Even if you're not in it?"

"Well, I can't say I wouldn't *prefer* that I was there with you, but yes. Even then." He loved the academy. And he knew Marcus loved it too. Whatever time Marcus wanted to spend here, Taemin was happy to let him.

Preeti looked between them. "Well," she said after a second, shouldering her backpack. "I should probably head out. Early class tomorrow. Speaking of early." She nodded at Marcus. "Don't let him stay out to late. Wednesday is a sparring morning."

"Got it," Marcus said, looking altogether too serious for what was obviously just a playful joke.

"Preeti, honestly."

She held up her hands. "Hey, I'm the one leaving. So I'm not the one keeping you up." Then, before he could say anything else, she said, "G'night sir, g'night Marcus! Text me!" And she turned tail and fairly ran out of the office.

"Let me know when you've gotten home safe!" Taemin called after her, the only reply being the bells over the door jingling as she left.

Taemin blinked in her wake. Preeti didn't usually linger too long on Tuesday nights because it was true, they both did have early mornings, but she usually didn't leave in quite such a rush. He looked to Marcus, who made a helpless gesture. "Don't look at me," he said. "For all I know, she's like that all the time."

Taemin chuckled. "She's something all right. I'm lucky to have kept her on."

Marcus nodded. "It seems like she really looks out for you. She and Mr. Avi both."

Taemin sighed. "Sometimes too much. I endure a lot of mother-henning." Though that did remind him.... He went and grabbed one of the boxes of snacks that had been left for him and pulled out a strawberry-flavored protein bar. Eating. He should do that. "Do you mind if I eat something quickly?"

Marcus shook his head. "No, please. And I don't want to keep you from your real dinner or anything. I just, you know. I wanted to see you one more time today. See how you were doing."

"Oh," Taemin said. "Thank you." He turned the protein bar over in his hands. "I appreciate it."

"Of course." *Of course.* Said so easily. Matter-of-factly. As though Marcus really didn't want to do anything else but be with him.

Reading too much into things. And he needed to stop.

"Well," he said, trying for bright, "I think we both do probably need to head out. I can walk you to your car."

"Do you mind if I stay while you close up?" Marcus sounded so *caring.*

Taemin had to look away. "Of course not."

Closing up only consisted of Taemin gathering all the attendance cards together and setting them on his desk to deal with the next day, putting on his shoes, and then grabbing his duffel bag and hitting the lights, Marcus following while Taemin locked up.

They faced each other in the dark of the parking lot. Taemin felt the need to say something, but he wasn't sure what.

After all, what *could* he say?

"Have a good night." He reached out to touch Marcus on the shoulder. "Drive safe, okay?"

Marcus touched his hand with his own, fingers curling around Taemin's, before he stepped back. "Yeah. You too."

Taemin smiled at him before going over to his own car. He gripped his steering wheel and took a deep breath before he started his car and drove to his apartment. He focused on the drive, tried to keep a lid on the thoughts churning in his head. He wanted….

He *wanted.*

He got to his complex, parked his car, and headed up the stairs. Kicked off his shoes and dropped his duffel. What was wrong with him? He shouldn't be feeling like this. He shouldn't be wanting Marcus like this.

But—

But today had definitely solidified his feelings. He'd needed someone and Marcus had been there, offering. And had gone the extra mile then, coming by the academy to check on him one more time.

All Taemin wanted out of someone to love was someone to *have.* To talk to, to come home to. To hold and be held by.

It'd only been a week.

God, it felt like so much longer.

He forced himself to go about his nightly routine but eventually found himself sitting up in bed staring down at his phone, scrolling through the text conversations he'd had with Marcus over the last several days. Even just reading the messages made him happy. Something about being with Marcus made Taemin feel light.

He set down his phone and lay down, pulling up the covers. Tried to will himself to sleep.

And not think about what Marcus looked like when he smiled.

MARCUS GOT home to his short-stay apartment and flipped on the light, surveying the bland modern decorations before he sighed.

Taemin's apartment was so much brighter. So full of life, and of him, and everything he cared about and stood for.

Marcus had gotten to go to Taemin's apartment to hold him today. And he'd been thanked for it. So many times, so quietly, that it felt like Marcus had taken something he shouldn't have.

If this guy really is as special as you think he is, even if he had to turn you down, I don't think he'd want you out of his life. That's—that's worth keeping in mind.

Billy knew what he was talking about. Taemin wasn't the sort who would be… disgusted. Confused maybe, taken aback for sure, but he wouldn't—he probably wouldn't tell Marcus not to let the door hit him on the way out.

It's just—it's not like Marcus could help it. Taemin was so… kind, understanding, encouraging—

Beautiful.

He had a smile that lit up the world, and a drive to help others so fierce that he'd built his life around it. He was strong and graceful and gorgeous, and Marcus couldn't *help* but be in love with him. It was so easy. Too easy.

Fuck, Billy was right. Marcus needed to stop *waffling*. He had made the decision a week ago, when he first saw Taemin back on that mat and everything had slammed into him, that he was going to do something about his feelings. He had made the decision over the weekend that he was going to ask Taemin out. He just needed to wait for the right time.

And he had made the decision hours ago that he wanted to be there for Taemin whenever he could. Hold him close, kiss his hair, tell him things would be okay.

Okay. Okay, okay, okay. He could do this. He *would* do this. He was a fucking leading man in the movie industry. He was famous, successful, and wealthy. He had *scores* of people dying to date him.

And none of that mattered to Taemin.

Marcus rubbed a hand over his face. Okay. He was going to try to woo the most genuine, down-to-earth human being on the planet.

In fact, he didn't have to woo, because this wasn't some fucking romantic flick; this was real life, with a real human person, and one Marcus cared about so much that the idea of messing up and doing the wrong thing was terrifying.

He could do this, though. He just needed to start small. All he had to do was ask. That was it.

"I'm interested in you," he said aloud, trying to get a feel for the words. "I'd like to date you. Maybe see where things go, if you felt like I was someone you might be interested in."

Simple, easy, to the point. Things Taemin would appreciate. He hoped.

WEDNESDAY WAS so busy for Taemin that he barely had any time to deal with inner turmoil, which was a nice upside to the fact that he was in constant motion from five in the morning to near ten that night.

He worked steadily through, managed a nap after working with the homeschool co-op, actually remembered to eat something when he woke up, and then it was time to go back to the academy to get ready for that evening's classes.

His phone buzzed just as he was unlocking the door, so he pulled it out to check it as he stepped out of his shoes, thinking it might be Mr. Avi, who worked Wednesday nights with him.

It wasn't; it was a message from Marcus, saying, *Hope the day's been treating you well so far. I've been in script reads and character prep all day. Some actual physical stuff too, though, which has been nice. Please tell me no if I'm being a bother, but I was hoping maybe I could come by tonight after class? I know you must be beat by then, and I promise I won't take up too much of your time. I just wanted to see you.*

I'd be happy to see you, Taemin replied, even as typing it twisted him into knots. Maybe if he were a stronger person he'd be able to put some distance between them, but he couldn't help wanting to see Marcus again.

Just—just wanting him close.

Classes passed a little slower than they usually did, and by the adult class, Mr. Avi was eyeing him with an expression Taemin knew to recognize as concern.

"Is something wrong, Mr. Avi?" he asked as they waited for their students to get on their sparring gear for the last fifteen minutes of class before cooldown.

"No, sir," Mr. Avi said after a moment. "Nothing much. How's the week been for you so far?"

"About the same as it always is. Busy, but positive. How's Julia? Is she feeling better?"

"Oh yeah, right as rain now."

"Good to hear."

"Yeah…." Mr. Avi seemed to consider something, then asked, "How did Sunday go?"

"Sunday?"

"Yeah, when you went out with Marcus. He actually talk you into slowing down a little?"

Sunday they had met for coffee and had ended up talking for so long that they went out to lunch too. Marcus had gotten recognized three times over the course of it, and he'd apologized each time, like he was the one being the burden when it was someone else intruding on their time. He'd also insisted on paying again, which Taemin only allowed because of how much it seemed to make Marcus happy. They'd only said their goodbyes when Taemin couldn't put off leaving for Detroit any longer, if he hadn't wanted to be late. "It was a very pleasant way to spend some time," he ended up saying.

"Good to hear. He tell you about how his work is going?"

"It hadn't really started when we met on Sunday, but we talked a little about it Monday, and then yesterday. It seems to be going well. Apparently filming will be starting this coming Monday."

Mr. Avi glanced at him, then turned back to the students who were starting to line up. "You've seen him a lot this week, huh?"

Taemin nodded, tried not to think too much about it. "I think I said before that it's been very nice, him making so much time to see me."

"Uh-huh." The last of their students had gotten back into the line, standing at attention, so the conversation was dropped to referee and have teaching matches.

MARCUS TRIED to time his arrival at the academy just as classes let out so he wouldn't be too much of a distraction but still didn't show up too late. He was lucky in that he bowed into the building as everyone else was grabbing up duffel bags and backpacks and heading out. A bright side to the adult class: most of them didn't have to wait around to be picked up.

"Hey," Mr. Avi said, coming over to him. He was holding the large push broom used to sweep the mat. "Nice to see you again."

Marcus smiled at him, trying to mask his nerves. "Thanks."

"Master Choi's going over attendances in his office," Mr. Avi said, nodding in the direction of the open door. "He probably didn't hear you come in over the noise of everyone else leaving."

Okay. Marcus didn't want to disturb him while he was working. He could say hi in a minute. Instead, he motioned at the broom. "Want me to take that off your hands?"

Mr. Avi's eyebrows went up. "You're a bigshot now and you want to sweep?"

"Hey, I'm not that much of a bigshot that I don't care about where I came from."

"All right, all right." Mr. Avi handed over the broom, and Marcus got to work.

He swept in silence for a minute or two before Mr. Avi came up to him, arms crossed. "You're totally gone on him, aren't you, kid?"

Marcus almost dropped the broom. "What?"

Mr. Avi just looked at him. "Master Choi. You basically haven't left him alone since you got here."

Marcus went cold. "Have I—has he said anything about me bothering him?" Had he pushed himself on Taemin, and Taemin had just been too polite to say no? He'd never forgive himself if he'd done something to make Taemin uncomfortable.

"Quit beating yourself up," Mr. Avi said. "He's done nothing but say how much he's enjoyed your company."

"Oh." Marcus nearly sighed in relief. "I'm glad to hear that."

"Yeah, I'll just bet you are. So? What's going on?"

"Exactly what you think is going on," Marcus said, turning his attention back to sweeping. He could talk and sweep at the same time, and it also meant he wouldn't have to make too much eye contact.

"Which is? Spell it out for me."

Marcus swallowed. Mr. Avi was close to Taemin, Marcus respected him on top of that, and so his opinion was important. Marcus needed to be careful in what he said and how he said it. "I really like him. I care about him a lot."

"After a week?"

"I know," Marcus said. "I know. But I can't help it. He's just…." *Perfect.* "He means a lot to me."

Mr. Avi sighed. "It's been ten years, kid."

"I know," Marcus said again. But on this he was sure. "It's been ten years, and after a week I know he's just as amazing as he was then. Better. I've had time to get over being starstruck. Now I've spoken to him adult to adult. Even ground." *And loving him is easy.* "And I know that I want to try."

"Try what?"

He stopped sweeping to meet Mr. Avi's eyes. "Making him happy. In whatever way I can do that."

Mr. Avi looked at him for a long time, gaze sweeping up and down. Marcus felt like he was being graded. At last Mr. Avi nodded, dropping his arms to his sides. "I knew Julia was it for me the moment I laid eyes on her. You *have* been making him happy this last week.

And I saw you on Saturday. It's about damn time he had someone in his life who looks at him the way you do."

"How's that?" Marcus couldn't help but ask.

Mr. Avi huffed a laugh. "Like he's your leading man."

Chapter Eight

"FLOOR'S SWEPT," Mr. Avi said, poking his head into Taemin's office.

Taemin looked up from his computer. "Oh! Thank you. I'll go get the mop. Are you heading out?"

"Yeah," Mr. Avi said as Taemin followed him out of the office. "Also, you've got a visitor."

Taemin felt equal parts delight and dread to see Marcus standing on the mat.

"Hi," he said with a little wave, smile small but bright. "How's the day been?"

Better, now that I get to see you. "Good," Taemin said, trying to sound cheerful.

"Okay," Mr. Avi said, "I'm taking off. 'Night you two."

They both said goodnights, and Mr. Avi waved before leaving the dojang, door jingling as it closed behind him.

"Did you want to talk now?" Taemin said, after a moment of them just looking at each other. "We can go into the office."

Marcus shook his head. "Mr. Avi said you mop on Wednesdays. I don't want to keep you from that. It's already been a crazy long day for you."

"It's okay. Mopping doesn't take very long." It was mostly to put a layer of disinfectant on the mat. He did it once a week, with an additional sweeping done on Monday, just to keep up the cleanliness of the dojang. "In fact, I can do it tomorrow even, as long as I give it enough time before classes start to let it dry."

"Oh no, I—I don't want to put you off your schedule."

Taemin chuckled. "It's okay. It's good to change things up once in a while. Come on, we can go talk now." He turned toward the office.

"Wait—" Marcus put a hand on his shoulder. "Wait, I—I can say it now."

Taemin obligingly turned back around. Marcus sounded nervous. "Is everything okay?"

Marcus blew out a breath. "God, I—I hope so."

"Marcus?" Taemin searched his face, concerned. "What's wrong?"

"Nothing. Nothing at all. I just—" Marcus swallowed and then said, "I really, really like you, Taemin. I was hoping you'd let me take you out. On a real date. One we both acknowledged as a date. If you were maybe interested in seeing where things might go."

Taemin's breath caught. "What?"

Marcus smiled at him, expression so soft it made Taemin ache. "It's okay if you don't feel the same way. I've really enjoyed just being a part of your life again and having you be a part of mine. I want to keep having that however you'll let me, if it's okay with you."

"No—I—" Taemin made an aborted motion to touch before pulling his hand back. Was this really—was Marcus offering—was this something he could *have*? "I—you—you like me? You'd want… you'd want to try having more?"

Marcus reached out and took Taemin's hand, meeting his eyes before pressing a kiss to his knuckles. "I want as much as you're willing to give. No more or less than that."

Taemin took a shaky breath. "Then yes. Yes, please. I—yes."

"Could I kiss you?" Marcus asked, voice a hoarse whisper.

Taemin swallowed and nodded, barely daring to believe it.

Marcus's free hand was warm against Taemin's cheek, and Taemin's eyes slid shut as Marcus leaned down. The brush of lips over his own was warm and soft, and Taemin couldn't help his free hand going to rest on Marcus's shoulder, clutching him tight as Marcus moved closer and deepened the kiss.

It was minutes later before Marcus pulled back. Just enough that they could look into each other's eyes. "Hey," he murmured.

Taemin couldn't help but smile and press another kiss to the corner of his mouth before he rested his head against Marcus's chest. Marcus's arms immediately came up to wrap around him.

It was safe and warm and perfect.

MARCUS HAD gotten to tell Taemin how he felt, and Taemin had looked at him with such wonder that it almost hurt. He'd gotten to kiss him and now was holding him and he basically never wanted to move.

But they couldn't stand there in the middle of the mat all night.

"It's late," Marcus said eventually, though he was loath to do so. "You've had a long day. You should really get home."

Taemin's hands tightened in his shirt and then let go before he took a step back. Marcus already missed his warmth, but it *was* late. He knew Taemin had been up since five and had gone hard pretty much all day. "I know you're right." Taemin sighed. "I just don't want to say good night yet."

Marcus chuckled. "Me neither. But we both have lots to do tomorrow." He was spending the entire day working on fight choreography, in between looking over the script. His day out of days was supposed to be released tomorrow, too, so he'd be talking to Billy about his schedule for the upcoming week.

"And Friday," Taemin said ruefully. "Saturday too, until I'm done with classes. But… maybe Saturday afternoon if you're free?"

"Absolutely," Marcus said quickly. "Yes. After your last class ends at one?"

Taemin bit his lip, obviously torn. "I really should spend at least another hour on the mat after class, just to get some more practice in."

"How about this," Marcus said. "I'm not working Saturday. Won't be, until we really begin filming next week. How about I come in for the specialty training class and I do the best I can to give you a run for your money? And then we can do something after. You already do the conditioning class in the morning, right? So with that and time with me, you'll get at least some training out of it."

Taemin blinked. "I—I guess that'd be okay."

"Okay," Marcus said warmly. "We've got a plan, then."

Taemin smiled at him. "A good one, even."

Marcus moved to cup Taemin's cheek, unable to help himself, and his breathing went ragged when Taemin closed his eyes and nuzzled into his hand. "God, it's going to feel like forever until I can see you again."

"We'll both be busy," Taemin said, eyes still closed. "It'll help time pass faster."

"If you say so." Marcus trailed his hand down the side of Taemin's face before leaning down to press one more kiss to his lips. "I'll see you Saturday, okay?"

Taemin nodded. "Saturday."

"Okay." Marcus stepped back. "Let's close up, then, yeah? So I know you're actually leaving to go home and get some rest."

Taemin made a face. "Honestly. No one trusts me to take care of myself."

"Nah, I know you can." *Mostly.* "It's just that I want to take care of you too."

"Oh."

Marcus smiled at him. "C'mon. Let's get your stuff and hit the lights."

They might have lingered in the parking lot just a little longer, but eventually they managed to say final goodnights, get into their own cars, and drive off.

Marcus didn't remember any of his drive to his apartment, and he made it inside in a daze. He'd already eaten, so it was only a matter of brushing his teeth and getting undressed before he was sliding into bed.

He lay back against his pillows and closed his eyes, breathing out. Fuck, he'd been *allowed.* Allowed to touch Taemin and not feel guilty, allowed to hold him, to *kiss* him—it was everything he'd been dreaming about since they'd first been reunited.

Marcus touched his fingers to his lips, remembering how Taemin had tasted. The quiet little sounds he'd made against Marcus's mouth.

He swallowed, picturing Taemin's eyes closed in pleasure. Maybe making more of those noises as Marcus touched him, ran his hands up and down Taemin's body.

His free hand crept lower, stroking down the flat planes of his stomach as he imagined touching Taemin the same way. Feeling him, strong and lean, honed from years of training. Marcus would do his level best to make Taemin come apart.

It would start with kissing him. Marcus really enjoyed kissing, and he knew he'd never get tired of Taemin's mouth, the velvety slide of lips and tongue. Maybe as they kissed, Taemin would let Marcus lay him down, would even arch up against him as Marcus elicited more sounds. God, just hearing them tonight….

He shuddered, overtaken with the image of Taemin gasping in pleasure as they moved together. As Marcus used his body, the body he'd worked so hard on, to make Taemin feel as good as he possibly could.

Marcus fisted a hand in the sheets and came with a groan, picturing himself coaxing Taemin into doing the same.

It was minutes before he managed to get his breathing back under control, the thought that he might one day be able to do more than just imagine leaving him winded all over again.

Only a week had passed, but he knew that this was something he wanted to *work.* To last.

He so hoped Taemin felt the same way.

TAEMIN'S THURSDAY was, to the outside eye, probably business as usual. He did get up and go to the academy, first to mop, then to do paperwork while he waited for the mat to dry. After, he did his own regular workout, headed home to shower and eat something quickly before he went right back out again to do his volunteer work of the day.

The only big change was how he felt, which was so happy that he might burst from it. Last night he hadn't had much more energy than to get home and drop into bed, the memory of Marcus's kisses and gentle smile easing him to sleep.

Now he was awake enough to really remember every detail, and just the phantom feeling of Marcus's warmth enveloping him was delicious.

Hope your day is going well, Marcus texted him around one fifteen, just as Taemin was leaving the hospital. *Missing you.*

Taemin propped himself up against his car to type back. *It's going very well. How are things on your end?*

Well it started out great, since I had a good memory to wake up to. And the choreography is a lot of fun to learn. Hard work, but I'm not afraid of that.

I know, Taemin replied, unable to help his smile. *You work very hard. It's very admirable.*

Stop, you'll make me blush.

It made Taemin grin, that Marcus was flirting. That it was done so easily. *I'm sure it's a good look on you*, he sent back. *What are you doing right now?*

Breaking to eat. Then I'm meeting up with Billy for scheduling stuff. He likes it when we actually sit down to go over things when we can, over doing things on the phone.

It sounds like he's very good at his job.

He's the best, Marcus sent. *I owe him a lot. It'd be cool if you met him at some point. I think you two'd get along.*

I'd be happy to!

And you? What are you doing right now?

I just finished with Kids Kicking Cancer, Taemin replied. *Now I have a little free time until classes begin this afternoon.*

Free time! That's a marvel.

I know, Taemin replied wryly. *But it'll be time well spent. Grocery shopping, for one thing.*

And then eating lunch after, right?

That was a good point. Taemin had planned to go grocery shopping and then maybe take a nap until he had to head over to the school, but he should probably fit lunch into his plans too. *Yes, and eating lunch.*

Good to hear. I should probably get my head back into the game now, though. Talk to you later?

Of course, Taemin sent. *Text me anytime. I'll reply when I can.*

Right back atcha.

Smiling, Taemin stowed his phone and got into his car, going straight home. He lived fairly close to a superstore and felt silly driving when he could simply walk. Since it was just him, he didn't have to buy a lot of groceries, especially not at one time. He usually just bought things as needed when he ran out, and the perishables he went through during the week.

His list today was fairly small, so he was in and out of the store in less than an hour. Then it was back to his building and up the stairs to put everything away.

He got distracted after that was done, because he needed to water his plants and vacuum, and then he decided that since he was vacuuming, it was probably a good time to start a load of laundry while he cleaned his bathroom. It was only once he'd put his clothes into the dryer that he remembered about actually eating lunch.

That was easy, though. He started his rice cooker, placing some broccoli in the steamer basket over it while the rice cooked, and pulled out some of the chicken he'd just bought and got that into a pan with some oil and seasoning. It cooked up pretty fast, and the rice wasn't too far behind, so soon enough he had a good, well-balanced lunch. Preeti would be proud.

Feeling a little mischievous, he even took a picture and sent it to her.

He got a *!!! good job Master Choi!!* a few minutes later, which made him snicker. And made him think of someone else who might appreciate the photo.

"HEY, BILLY," Marcus said, sitting down across from Billy in the Starbucks they'd agreed to meet at. "How's it going?"

"Not bad. Got some interview requests that I wanted to talk over with you." He raised an eyebrow. "Not a whole lot else, since you didn't want me at the gym today."

Marcus shrugged. "We'll be there a lot for the next few months. Figured you could use the first week off."

Billy rolled his eyes. "I'm not a wilting flower. And my literal job is to follow you around wherever you go."

"Unless I say otherwise."

"Yes," Billy said, exasperated, "unless you say otherwise. In *certain circumstances* because sometimes I overrule you, that also kind of being a part of my job, if I want to do it well."

"Which is why you've got the job in the first place." Marcus grinned.

"Oh my god, this is the dumbest conversation we've ever had. I'm coming to the gym with you tomorrow, and I will talk to very important people and not-so-important people on the phone and get you snacks when you want snacks. I don't have to have involved conversations with everyone in the damn gym."

"Okay, okay." Marcus held up his hands. "Your call."

"Yes. It is. Thank you." Billy took a sip of his latte. "Now then, to business, maybe? Could we do that?"

Marcus chuckled. "Yeah, okay, sure."

They had their heads bent together over the day out of days that outlined Marcus's tentative schedule for the next two weeks when Marcus's phone beeped. Billy went quiet while Marcus checked who it was from. Billy was the one who got most of Marcus's scheduling updates, but sometimes they went straight to Marcus. And Billy wasn't always the liaison between Marcus and the rest of the cast; Marcus was currently in conversation with a bunch of other people he'd be on set with, from Roger to Leo to Hailey (and her mom).

When he saw who it was from, though, he couldn't help a grin. Taemin had sent him a picture of a plate of food. *Lunch*, he'd written. *Photographic evidence. See? No reason to make a fuss.*

I appreciate the update, Marcus typed back. *You've accomplished a lot this day.*

Oh hush.

He sent back a couple emojis and then looked up to see Billy watching him. "What?"

Billy tilted his head. "Good news?"

"I—yeah. I talked to Taemin."

"Well," Billy said after a second, "you're beaming, so I'm guessing things went well?"

Marcus glanced back down at his phone. "Yeah. Yeah, really well."

"Good," Billy said vehemently. Marcus looked back up, startled at the ferocity of it. "I'm glad to hear that."

"It was halfway your advice that pushed me to do it," Marcus said honestly. "Thank you."

At that, Billy smirked. "See? I'm good at my job."

"And at being a friend."

"Okay, I guess that too." Billy shook his head. "But really. I'm happy for you. It's about damn time you found someone who makes you happy the way he obviously does."

"Thanks, Billy," Marcus said, touched.

"Mm-hm. I'd like to meet him, at some point. See for myself why you think he hung the damn moon."

Marcus laughed. "I already told him that I'd like you two to meet."

Billy blinked at him. "What, really?"

"Well, yeah, of course. You're both, you know, important people in my life. If nothing else, you can both complain about me."

"Oh," Billy said. He tapped his fingers on the table. "I guess I don't have *that* much to complain about."

"Love you too, Billy."

Billy rolled his eyes. Marcus was very used to that from him. "I'm happy for you. I look forward to meeting him. Back to work now, please."

FRIDAY WAS the usual busy-busy-busy for Taemin. A few weeks ago Fridays were actually one of his more restful days, since he didn't have anything to do but his own training and errands until the homeschool co-op at one. But now he had morning meetings in Ann Arbor to deal with too. Trials were getting closer and closer, so Taemin was scheduling as much extra practice in as he could.

It did mean that working with the homeschool co-op was a little more difficult, since he was so tired by the time one o'clock rolled around. He usually ended up going home to squeeze a nap in before heading back to the academy to get ready for classes, though, which helped.

Also, he and Marcus exchanged texts throughout the day. They were sporadic, as both of them were busy, but that just made each new one a nice surprise.

Looking forward to seeing you tomorrow, Marcus had sent around eight o'clock, while Taemin was in class. It was a good feeling to check his phone after class was over and find that.

Looking forward to seeing you too, he replied before heading home to shower and get ready for bed.

Under the covers, he couldn't help but think about what Saturday might bring. He'd get to see Marcus again, for one thing. Train with him, too, which would be fun. After—he didn't even care what they did. Even just sitting and talking together at the café on Sunday had been a wonderful time.

It was strange to think of Sunday. Not that long ago at all.

And now he had a date. With someone who understood him. Who got why he was so focused on his school, his work, and the volunteering that made up his life. Who didn't begrudge the hours he spent training. Who even offered to be a part of them. It was all he could have hoped for.

He had to rein himself in, with that thought. It *had* only been a week. Even if he could already see himself wanting something that would last, that was a little much—and very soon. The last thing he'd want to do was put any pressure on Marcus regarding a relationship.

Take one thing at a time. He knew he was bad at that; he tended to throw himself into things. But that wouldn't be fair to either of them. Better to just enjoy the moments and see how things went.

"HEY!" PREETI said, coming over to him as Marcus bowed into the dojang. She was holding her bo. "You're back!"

"Couldn't stay away," Marcus said easily. "But what are you doing here? I thought you didn't work Saturdays."

"I don't. But I was asked to do a last-minute demonstration for a Girl Scout troop tomorrow. Wanted to just go over my bo routine in a place that had mirrors."

"Gotcha." He waved to Taemin and Mr. Avi when they glanced over at him. Mr. Avi nodded before turning back to the students he was working with. It looked as though they were practicing poomsae, the forms that required exact steps and careful movements. Taemin, though, in full sparring gear already, came over to him.

"Hey," Marcus said, smiling softly.

"Afternoon," Taemin said brightly. God, he looked amazing. "Thank you for coming."

"Of course. Looking forward to giving you a run for your money."

"And I'm very much looking forward to seeing you try," Taemin replied with a grin.

Preeti glanced back and forth. "Oh," she said at last. "You're why Master Choi is in sparring gear, huh?"

"Yep. Said I'd show him what I could do."

"Okay, cool. Well, uh, you guys have fun."

"Don't worry." Marcus grinned.

She gave him a funny look but went back to an empty part of the mat to do her bo practice.

"Preeti seems suspicious," Taemin said quietly, as they walked over to grab Marcus's gear.

Marcus had to laugh. "No kidding. Pretty sure she knows what's up. Mr. Avi already does."

"He does?"

Marcus nodded. "He didn't, uh, quite give me the shovel talk Wednesday night before you and I figured things out, but it wasn't too far off from that."

Taemin blinked, eyes wide. "Oh."

"Does it bother you?" Marcus asked hesitantly. "That they might know?"

Taemin shook his head. "Not really. It's a little odd, I'll admit. But I have no intention to hide the fact that we're, um…."

"Going to try going out," Marcus finished. Simple and no pressure, which was exactly how he wanted things to go.

Taemin smiled at him. "Yes."

"All right, then. We'll just take things as they come, yeah?"

"I think that sounds very good." Taemin held out the chest protector. "Now, I think you said something about giving me a run for my money?"

Marcus laughed and geared up, and then he and Taemin headed to an empty part of the mat. "How do you want to time it?" Taemin asked.

"Your call. Want to just go for points? Stop once one of us reaches twelve?" He was confident they'd both be able to keep track in their heads.

"Works for me," Taemin said. "Ready?"

"Ready."

They both put in their mouth guards, bowed, and began.

It was, Marcus realized almost as soon as they started, *no freaking contest.* He was pretty good; great shape, decent stamina. But Taemin was a machine. It was all Marcus could do to block half his hits and circle to stay in the ring. He tried to keep it up for as long as he could, but it was almost sad how quickly those twelve points added up.

Taemin hopped back and then held up a hand, signaling that he'd totaled the match. Marcus dropped his hands and took out his mouth guard. "All right," he said. "One, you're incredible. Two, when we sparred last Thursday, exactly how easy were you taking it on me?"

Taemin took out his own mouth guard. Grinning, he said, "Not *too* easy?"

Fucking hell. "Well, there's a reason you're an Olympic hopeful."

"Ready to go again?"

Yes, yes he was. Seeing Taemin move in his element like this? He was amazing. "Of course. I promised you a workout. Got to at least keep you moving."

Taemin chuckled and popped his mouth guard back in.

They went hard for what must've been a good ten minutes before Taemin called time for them both to grab some water. Marcus definitely appreciated the breather, but at least—to his credit, he felt—he didn't need to tap out completely.

"Are you sure?" Taemin asked, when Marcus said he was ready to go again.

"Yup. Can't count me out just yet. Even if I can't score on you, I can damn well make sure to keep your cardio up."

Taemin beamed at him. "Sounds good to me."

Chapter Nine

MARCUS HAD definitely worked hard over the years; Taemin could tell. He had fantastic reflexes and was able to block a good majority of Taemin's hits, even if it was clear he wasn't as used to being in the ring. Marcus had mentioned a lot of real-world practice. Taemin would have to ask him about that. If Marcus had the time, maybe he could even be a guest at a specialty training hour.

For now, though, after nearly forty-five minutes—with a fifteen-minute break in between—Taemin called full time so that they could both cool down. Marcus staggered a little when he went over to a corner to remove his gear. "I am definitely going to be feeling this tomorrow," he groaned.

Taemin had to laugh. "You were the one who said you'd give me a workout."

"Ugh."

Taemin laughed again and went to start class cooldown, Marcus joining in as soon as he put away the last of his pads. He was feeling a little shaky himself, now that the adrenaline had worn off some, but it was nothing some rest and a meal wouldn't fix.

As the class said their goodbyes, a few of them—Jamal and Roshen included—went up to Marcus. Taemin wasn't able to hear their questions, but Marcus nodded along to them. When Taemin went over to see what they were talking about, he caught the tail end of "—picture? My friends don't believe me."

"Sure," Marcus said easily. "Now?"

"If that's okay?"

"Are you being hounded again?" Taemin asked, stepping forward.

Roshen turned to him, eyes wide. "Sorry, sir. I'm just—he said it was okay—"

"It's all right," Marcus said, waving a hand. "You wanna get your phone?"

"Thank you!"

"And no more after this," Taemin said sternly. "This is a dojang, not a fan club. He's a student just like you. Understand?"

They both nodded. "Yessir."

After the pictures had been taken and Jamal and Roshen left for Jamal's car, Taemin turned back to Marcus. "I'm really sorry. It's not right."

"It's okay," Marcus said. "I'm used to it. I'm more sorry that it disrupted your environment. Um. It's been great this last week, but with Roshen most likely posting that picture all over social media, it's possible that you might get some people coming in just to see if they can spot me." He sighed. "It'll probably be better if I don't come to any more actual classes."

Taemin nodded. "I'll be sorry to miss you, but I understand. We can still make time for each other outside of classes."

Marcus's lips quirked. "Even though you live here?"

"I make time for what is important to me," Taemin said, matter-of-fact. His life was busy, it was true, but Marcus was worth making time for. If Marcus didn't mind spending some time with him before or after a workday, of course Taemin was willing to stay up a little later or get up a little earlier. And he still had pockets of time on Saturday after classes and Sunday around training. He could do it.

"Oh." Marcus blinked. "Yeah. Okay."

"Okay." Taemin grinned.

"Um," Preeti said, from where she was standing a few feet back off the mat, bo in hand and shoes on. "Sorry to interrupt?"

"You're fine," Taemin said, turning to her. "What is it?"

"Nothing! I just wanted to say goodbye before I took off."

Taemin smiled at her. "Have a good time at the demonstration."

"I will. Oh, and do you have any more flyers? I can take some with me to pass out."

"Sure. Come on. They're in my office. Marcus, I'll be right back, and then we can go?"

"Sounds great."

Taemin waved goodbye to Mr. Avi and then headed to his office, Preeti following him. As soon as they were inside, Preeti asked, "You mind if I close the door?"

Taemin looked at her in surprise. That meant she wanted a private conversation. "Of course. Is something wrong?"

She shook her head, twisting her fingers together. "Nosir."

Taemin raised an eyebrow at her expression. "But?"

"It's not any of my business," Preeti said quickly. "I'll, uh, I'll just take the flyers. Never mind."

"All right." He went over to his cabinet and riffled through it, pulling out a little bundle of flyers, which he handed over to her. "Anything else?"

She took them, shaking her head. "Nosir. Thank you."

As she shifted from foot-to-foot, Taemin took pity on her. "Preeti?"

"Yessir?"

"The answer to your question is yes. I trust that's not going to be a problem?"

Preeti burst into a grin. "No, sir!"

He matched her smile. "Good. Anything else?"

She shook her head again.

"All right, then. Why don't we get going?"

Once out of the office, Preeti made a beeline for Marcus, slapping him on the shoulder. "See you around!" she said cheerfully before she hurried out of the dojang.

Marcus blinked after her, then turned to Taemin. "Anything I should know?"

Taemin chuckled. "I think she's happy for us."

"Oh, you told her?"

"She pretty much guessed. I just confirmed her suspicions. Was that all right?"

"Sure. I mean, they're your people. The ones on my side already know too."

"Oh, yes?"

Marcus rubbed the back of his neck. "Might not have been able to really shut up about it. Though, uh, Billy is already talking about looking at it from a publicity standpoint. I—I hope that's okay with you."

"Why wouldn't it be?"

Marcus shrugged. "I, uh, I'm going to do my best to keep things quiet, but it's going to get out. That's just how things work. It's going to be a lot. I wanted to talk to you about it."

"Okay. So we can do that over lunch."

"Okay," Marcus said, sounding relieved.

"But for now, I think I'd like to go home and shower. You're welcome to one too."

"That'd be great, yeah."

"Then we can head out. Sound good?"

"Yeah." Marcus looked at him, then grinned wide. "Hey."

"Mm?"

"Could I get a kiss for the road?"

"Oh," Taemin said, flushing with pleasure. "I'd like that very much."

TAEMIN INSISTED Marcus get to have the shower first. Marcus did his best to jump in and out as quickly as possible, without thinking too much about the fact that he was naked in a place that *Taemin* was routinely naked.

He was not, altogether, too successful, and ended up turning the water cold to finish up before throwing on deodorant and his clothes and leaving the bathroom to let Taemin take his turn.

As he waited (and again, tried to avoid thinking about Taemin just a few feet away, under running water) he pulled out his phone and looked up places to eat. He had a couple in mind but wanted to see what Taemin was in the mood for.

Luckily he didn't have too long to wait and stew. Taemin emerged from his room, dressed in shorts and a fitted shirt—another Choi's one, Marcus thought with amusement. He wondered if Taemin had any other T-shirts at this point. He then proceeded to plop down on the couch next to Marcus and scoot in close. Marcus immediately put his arm around him, ridiculously pleased with this turn of events.

"Okay," he said. "I don't know about you, but I worked up an appetite. What are you in the mood for?"

"I picked last time," Taemin said. "It's your turn. But…." He bit his lip.

"Yeah?"

Taemin seemed to consider his words. "Would you like to maybe stay here and order in?"

"Sure. Any particular reason why?"

"I just feel bad about how often you get approached in public," Taemin said after a moment. "I thought that maybe it might be nice if it was just us for a little while. And you wouldn't have to worry about anyone else."

Touched, Marcus said, "I—yeah. Yeah, that'd be really nice. And this way I get you all to myself too."

"All right." Taemin smiled. "That's a plan. What would you like to get?"

Marcus laughed. "Okay, this is going to sound completely cliché, but would you mind pizza?"

"Not at all."

"Great! Have you heard of Cottage Inn? It's got great reviews."

"Sounds good to me."

They decided on what to order and Marcus placed it. "We've got some time 'til delivery," Marcus said, angling in toward Taemin.

Taemin smiled shyly at him. "I have an idea of how to pass the time."

Marcus smiled back, hopeful. "Yeah?"

In answer, Taemin moved forward to kiss him. Marcus eagerly pulled him closer to kiss back. They moved with each other until Taemin was practically in Marcus's lap, and Marcus reveled in the feel and taste of him. God, being able to trade kisses was *incredible.*

He pressed a kiss to the corner of Taemin's mouth and then moved to kiss under his jaw. Taemin's fingers flexed against him, and he made a high, thready sound that made Marcus go hot. *Fuck.* "That okay?"

In answer, Taemin surged forward to catch his mouth again, and Marcus shifted, changing the angle just a bit, to get a little more contact, hands roaming over Taemin's back. He brushed a sliver of skin at the base of Taemin's spine as his shirt rode up and Marcus couldn't help stroking that spot, feeling Taemin's warmth. He pulled back, just enough to ask, "I—can I—" *Touch you. Take just a little more.*

"Please do," Taemin murmured against Marcus's lips. His hand trailed down, hovered over the hem of Marcus's own shirt. "May I—?"

"God, yes," Marcus managed, even as he moved a hand fully underneath Taemin's shirt, taking in the feel of all that warm skin. Taemin moved impossibly closer, one hand gripping Marcus's bicep while the other slid underneath Marcus's tee, stroking over the planes of his stomach. Marcus couldn't help his gasp, and he accidentally nipped Taemin's lip.

Taemin moaned into it.

Which—just—

Marcus licked into Taemin's mouth before nipping again, tugging a little, exhaling shakily when Taemin made that noise again, before he shifted away. "Wait—"

Marcus froze, eyes widening. "Taemin?"

But Taemin only smiled at him. Darted in to kiss him, light and quick, before he leaned to pull off his shirt. "Okay?"

"Fuck, look at you," Marcus whispered, reaching for him. Taemin made a pleased noise and went.

They both shifted again, until Taemin was on his back, Marcus above him, and it was so much like Marcus's fantasy from before that he had to take a second to marvel, staring down at Taemin's beautiful, flushed face.

Taemin reached up to stroke down Marcus's cheek, Marcus shuddering and turning his head to press a kiss to Taemin's palm, before he leaned forward again.

The buzzer sounding out in the apartment was loud and startling, making Marcus jump.

Taemin looked at him ruefully. "Food's here."

Right. And they both *did* need to eat. "Yeah," Marcus sighed, pulling back and helping Taemin sit up.

Taemin grabbed his shirt from where it was lying on the floor and pulled it back over his head. Marcus squashed his disappointment at that but stood, going into the kitchen while Taemin went to answer the door. Marcus had already paid with tip, so Taemin only had to take the food as it was handed over.

"At least it smells good," Marcus grumbled, opening cabinets until he found the plates, going to set them on the table.

Taemin laughed softly. "It does. Let's eat. After all, you did want to have a conversation."

Right. And an important one too. Taemin had already experienced a little bit of Marcus's… audience, but Marcus really wanted to prep him about what he might be getting into.

And… and the possibility of Taemin deciding it might be too much…. Marcus didn't want to think about it, but it *was* a possibility. It was a lot for anyone, but Taemin was a quiet, dedicated man who already worked so hard to do what he did. The last thing Marcus wanted was to be a burden to him.

They served themselves, and Marcus waited until they'd both eaten at least a slice each (which they did, alarmingly fast—but not a surprise after how much they'd worked out). "So."

"So," Taemin agreed.

Marcus sighed. "There's no real humble way to say this, but… I'm kind of known, you know?"

Taemin nodded. "Even from what I've seen this past week, I understand."

"Yeah. And—and okay, uh, I know you don't really follow social media and stuff, which I don't blame you for. It can get kind of crazy. But people… care about me. And where I go. And who I date." Taemin nodded again. "So I—I guess I just want to know your thoughts on that. I really don't want to compromise on your privacy, but it, uh, it might be better to let the world know in a way we can control. Over it just leaking out."

"What else are you worried about?" Taemin asked. "I can tell there's something else."

Marcus averted his eyes. "The chance of things filtering into Choi's is… not small. Roshen and Jamal already know who I am, for instance. And Roshen's picture of me at the school, training there… that could blow up. Might already have, even if it was only like an hour ago."

"I see. All right. So what did you have in mind?"

"Well, not going live about that we're dating yet. I don't want to do that to you, especially not early on." *I want this to last, but I also want to keep you protected as long as possible.* "But regarding the academy, I want to at least talk to Billy—he also works on my publicity—about what we could do to avoid Choi's getting inundated with my fans."

"That makes sense. And as I said, I understand if that means you aren't able to actually train with me during classes. Though I will miss it, and I'm sure Preeti and Mr. Avi will too."

"Yeah." Marcus sighed. "I'd love to keep coming on Saturdays, but that might not be feasible anyway, with filming."

"You work weekends too?" Taemin asked, surprised.

"Not always, but the schedule changes. And with such a large production taking place in so many areas, we're kind of going to be shoving in as much time as we can in front of the camera. Days get long. I don't spend them all in front of the camera myself—stand-ins are used to check placement and lighting and all that, and other scenes are also being shot, so I won't be needed *every* day, not to mention

I'm required to get a certain amount of time off a week. But I still will be living on set, for the most part."

"Oh." Taemin sounded disappointed. "I supposed that might make seeing each other more difficult, especially since the weekend and some certain times during the day is mostly when I'm free."

Marcus shook his head. "We'll make it work. I want it to. Just like you said before—I can make time for something so important to me. And uh, I can talk to some people, see if I can't get certain days to start a little later. Maybe we could make Thursday morning time for us. You know, before you go to volunteer."

"I'd like that very much," Taemin said, smiling. "And you said you got your day out of days in, right?"

"Right. Tentative, but I know what I'm *supposed* to be doing and where I'm supposed to be doing it for the next two weeks."

"All right. Then let's look at our schedules now! We can figure out when we'll be able to actually see each other, and we can text and call in the meantime."

Marcus had to breathe a sigh of relief. Taemin understood. And still wanted to try to make this work. "Yeah, of course. Good idea."

HOW DO I look? Marcus sent to Taemin on Tuesday afternoon. He was wearing distressed jeans, a fitted red shirt, and a bomber jacket. He looked incredibly attractive, if a little overdressed for the middle of May. *You get the first sneak peek at my character's main outfit.*

You look very handsome, Taemin replied. *I'm sure your fan club will be very appreciative.*

I care less about their opinions and more about yours.

Taemin smiled at his phone and sent back a heart emoji.

He and Marcus wouldn't be able to see each other again until Thursday morning, but they would at least be able *to* see each other. Marcus didn't have to be on set until nine thirty, so he and Taemin were going to meet a little before eight to get an early breakfast. It did mean Taemin had to wake up earlier than he usually did on a

Thursday—especially after Wednesday, which was one of his longest days—because he usually preferred to do his morning training on an empty stomach, but that was fine with him, if it meant getting to see Marcus again.

They were texting back and forth all the time aside from that, just little snippets about each others' days. Taemin was learning a lot about how movie sets worked behind the scenes, thanks to Marcus's stories and pictures. It was all very interesting, though he could see it being incredibly overwhelming. Not for the first time, he found Marcus impressive—not only for doing what he did, but for how far he'd come, from barely being able to meet Taemin's own eyes.

For now, though, he'd just finished with Kids Kicking Cancer and was headed to Choi's to get some more training in. Then he'd eat, then go back to Choi's. Preeti was coming in at about three to train herself before classes; they were going to drill poomsae and bo.

He was looking forward to the break poomsae practice would provide. It was much more deliberate movement, over strength, stamina, and cardio training. And while performance poomsae had to be done at a certain speed, training them could still be very meditative. That would be nice. He was feeling more tired than usual lately, and the thought of Wednesday made him antsy in a way he was unused to. But it was such a long day, starting early and ending so late, and then he'd be getting up early on Thursday, too, when he normally was able to sleep in a little.

He shook his head. No, it'd be fine. He knew what he could handle, and he'd always managed working hard. Granted, all the new additions to his routine all at once—his Olympic training, Marcus—it was more than he had ever done at the same time.

But Taemin had things he wanted to do and people he wanted to see and spend time with, and that was that.

"OKAY," LEO said, jumping back to his feet. "After you stand, then you step back." He did so. "Left arm comes back, bam, hammer fist to the face, complete the spin." He followed through with the motions as he talked. "And right arm comes up for the next punch."

"Got it," Marcus said, stepping up and nodding to Daniel, the stuntman who was getting a hammer fist to the face. "Ready?"

Danny saluted and moved into fighting stance, before they started the routine from the top. As fight sequences went, it wasn't super complicated, but it was on the longer side, and a bunch of different takes were going to be needed to cover all the angles so the editors could do the best job possible in the cutting room.

"Time, guys," Leo said, clapping, after what must've been the sixth run-through of the whole routine. "You guys break for now, and I'll work with the aerialists." They were using some for the fighting in antigravity bits. The current team all nodded, slapped each other on the backs, and went to go grab water bottles and snacks, some of the more geared-up guys taking off masks or helmets to get some air.

"Here," Billy said, coming up to him with a water bottle in one hand and a smoothie in the other. "Intersperse."

"Thanks," Marcus said, grabbing the bottle and uncapping it. He downed a third of it before switching his attention to the smoothie. It was barely melted. "How'd you even know to have this ready?"

Billy looked affronted. "Um? I'm good at my job?"

Marcus raised an eyebrow.

"Seriously. There's a place just a couple minutes down the road, and I could tell you guys would be winding down sooner over later. I just ducked out to grab it, then stored it in the fridge. Easy."

"Thanks," Marcus said again. "And how're you doing? Bored yet?"

Billy rolled his eyes. "Please. I've my phone, my tablet, and an internet connection. I'm moving mountains."

Marcus grinned. "No doubt about that."

"Reset, Veronica!" Leo called up to the girl who was acting as Hailey's stunt double. Veronica was a Michigan find and actually one of the students at the gym. She and Hailey had approximately the same build, which was very good for a child actor. Hailey was a small eleven playing nine, while Veronica was thirteen. They were already behaving like siblings—the kind that got along. Veronica nodded, and Leo climbed up the rope next to her, calling to the man who was playing the bad guy in the scene.

Marcus watched Billy track Leo as he scaled the rope before he frowned, lips twisting, and turned back to Marcus. "So," he said. "How did this morning go?"

Marcus couldn't help a smile. "Really nice." They'd talked a lot about Marcus's work, which Taemin had taken an active interest in. Marcus was happy to share. On Taemin's end, his trials were next Saturday, and he was going to be flying out Friday morning to get settled in before the tournament. He was clearly bursting with excitement about it—a mix of not feeling ready yet and wanting things to hurry up and get started. Marcus had been able to share the sentiment of just working in film in general, but he'd really wanted to focus on what a big, important moment this was for Taemin. He said as much to Billy.

"It's pretty impressive that he's made it as far as Olympic tryouts."

"I know," Marcus enthused. "He's really spectacular. You should see him spar—he wiped the floor with me. It was incredible."

Billy snorted. "Only you would get this excited about being beaten up."

"I'm serious! I could barely touch him. And I'd like to think I'm in pretty good shape."

"You are literally a movie star famous for his fight scenes," Billy said dryly. "I'd *hope* you were in good shape. Which, I do suppose makes him even more impressive."

"Absolutely."

"And you're seeing him again…?"

"Sunday afternoon," Marcus said, already wishing it were sooner. "He's doing an exhibition Saturday evening, and I wanted him to have some time in between to decompress. And nap." Hopefully. Taemin had said he'd be happy to see Marcus on Saturday after classes and before his exhibition, but that would have given him absolutely no rest time. Time to yourself was important, especially with such a high-intensity, high-interactive job like Taemin had. Marcus knew from experience that going so long would just result in a drop. Often when you least wanted one.

Privately, Marcus felt that Taemin was pushing himself too hard. It might have worked for him up 'til now, but Marcus doubted even Taemin had trained with such ferocity before. Now, with such a big competition coming up, and Taemin also all of a sudden trying to make time to spend with Marcus… that was a lot. So even if Taemin *could* have made time for Marcus on Saturday, Marcus felt the need to step back.

"That makes sense," Billy said, after Marcus explained that. "Sounds like he does kind of overwork himself."

"I don't think it'd be as bad if he took, like, *breaks.* But he doesn't, as far as I can tell"—and as far as Marcus had learned from conversations with Mr. Avi and Preeti—"he just pushes through."

Billy frowned. "That's not going to end well, if he keeps it up."

"I know." But what could he do about it? He'd only been back in Taemin's life for a few weeks now. Even if Marcus was worried, he didn't know if it was really his place yet to say anything. Preeti and Mr. Avi seemed to be covering that anyway.

Not that Taemin appeared to listen.

"I know," he said again. "I'll just have to… keep an eye on it, I guess. See if I can't do anything to make things easier."

Billy smirked. "You could always offer to take a nap *with* him."

Marcus averted his eyes. It wasn't as though he hadn't thought about it. "Uh-huh."

"To actually sleep, of course."

"Right."

"After, you know, you tired him out."

Marcus coughed. Things he had been thinking about a lot since that first kiss… and last Saturday, on the couch, had only made those thoughts more colorful. He'd definitely been loath to say good night and leave.

Last Sunday Taemin had a seminar he was attending in the morning, followed by a meeting in Detroit after, so they had gone out for dinner together, but that was it. No kissing in public, especially not yet. Which was a good thing, because Marcus had been approached in the parking lot as they were saying their goodbyes. Same rule applied to breakfast that morning. Which meant Marcus had barely touched Taemin *since* Saturday. Wouldn't get to again until Sunday.

So yeah. He'd been spending a lot of time with his thoughts. And memories. And imagination.

Chapter Ten

SATURDAY WAS a long day for Taemin. It went fine, of course; classes ran smoothly, and the exhibition was fun. But it was still draining. He didn't even do any training on his own after classes, wanting to save his energy for the exhibition.

And maybe in hindsight he shouldn't have agreed to it with the Olympic trials so close, but he had been able to handle it. Besides, it was over now. He ached, the kind of bone-deep exhaustion that came from working a touch too hard, but that was nothing some sleep wouldn't solve. It was pretty early still, but he was about ready to drop, so he went home intending to go straight to bed.

He didn't have the energy to make a real dinner, but he was too tired to be hungry. He could hear almost everyone in his life yelling at him about it, though, so he grabbed a protein bar and forced that down before he went to take a shower. He spent too long under the spray, head resting against the tiled wall, not wanting to get out. The water was warm and soothing and—

He shook himself awake and got out of the shower.

After drying off, Taemin made a beeline for his bed, and, after a quick debate, set his alarm for a little later than he had been doing in the last couple months. He was going to Detroit to train in the morning instead of the afternoon in order to spend some more time with Marcus, so he didn't *really* need to wake up earlier for his own workout. He'd sleep in a bit and then work twice as hard in Detroit. The rest would probably be good for him. Trials were next week. He needed to be on his game. That meant resting when his body needed rest.

Marcus had sent him a few texts during the day that Taemin had replied to sporadically, and his last one had been sent around eight. *Looking forward to seeing you tomorrow :) Get some rest.*

Right. Taemin planned to. Tomorrow was another full day, but it would be a good one. He enjoyed training, and this was his last major meeting before next Saturday. And then he'd get to see Marcus. Taemin was going to pick up Chinese on his way back from Detroit, and they were going to do lunch at Taemin's place again. Mostly because they'd both wanted the option to be a little closer, and that wasn't something they could do in public. And it would also cut down on the people bothering Marcus for autographs and pictures—or even just stopping him to ask if he really was Marcus Economidis.

And after they'd eaten, they had the entire rest of the day just to be with each other. Maybe watch another of Marcus's movies, because it was pretty fascinating to see him onscreen. Or something that Marcus recommended, since Taemin was terrible at media. Or just to talk. To cuddle. Taemin really enjoyed tactility. Even holding hands was something he enjoyed. The last time they'd been alone together had been so special for so many reasons. He'd had *Marcus* and—intimacy. Just touching and being touched.

Taemin couldn't pretend he wasn't hoping for that again.

Maybe for more.

NO ONE on Earth could have blamed Marcus for how much his mind wandered on Sunday morning. From his workout to breakfast to getting together with Leo to shoot the shit, his mind was definitely focused on how soon he'd be seeing Taemin again.

"Man," Leo said after he'd had to repeat himself for the third time. "You are *out* of it today. What's going on?"

Marcus shook his head. "Nothing. I'm just looking forward to getting to see Taemin." But he couldn't help his grin.

Leo laughed. "Honeymoon phase has hit you hard, my friend."

"Yeah, maybe. I'm perfectly entitled. It's only been a couple weeks."

Leo shook his head. "I've known you for four years. You've never had it this bad before. This is something serious, yeah?"

Marcus's grin only grew. "Yeah."

Leo laughed again, big and booming. "How soon should we plan on wedding bells, huh?"

"Okay, for *that* it's a little early." *Think with the head and not with the heart, self.* It'd only been a few weeks. The relationship was still so new, it wasn't right to be thinking of that sort of future. Even if Taemin was everything Marcus could ever want.

Leo blinked, then looked at him hard. "Man, fuck. I wasn't being serious. But you are, aren't you?"

Marcus shrugged, trying for nonchalant but knowing he'd been caught out. They both made their livings reading body language. And Leo knew Marcus pretty well, after all this time. "I'm not trying to make things more than they are right now. If nothing else, that puts way too much pressure on something that we're both just trying to get a feel for."

"And yet?"

Marcus sighed. "And yet."

"Wow," Leo said after a moment. "I, uh, congratulations, I guess. That's pretty big. That you feel this way. It's... you haven't really, have you? Before."

Marcus shook this head. "I'm probably more serious about this than I've been about anything. Definitely in terms of a relationship." He'd met people on set before that he'd liked, who he'd had fun with. But, "We just click. In a way I never have with someone."

Leo nodded, a faraway look in his eyes. "All right. All right. Well. That's great."

"Thanks, Leo."

"YOU MADE it," Taemin said as he ushered Marcus into his apartment. "Welcome."

"Hey," Marcus said with a smile before he leaned down to kiss him hello. Taemin tilted his face up for the kiss, thrilled at the ease of it. How natural it seemed for Marcus to do so. "Thanks for having me over."

"Please. Of course. I'm so happy to see you again."

"Yeah," Marcus said, looking at him with such warmth. "Same here."

Taemin had texted Marcus as he picked up their food, before he started home, so Marcus had only arrived a little after Taemin did. It meant everything was still warm. Taemin had already set the table. "How was your day so far?"

"Great. Easy. And a nice last hurrah of free time, considering that full-on filming starts tomorrow."

"What did you do?" Taemin asked as they started to serve themselves.

"Just some puttering around in the morning, and then I met up with Leo. We work together but are pretty good friends outside of the set. It's kinda nice to see him when we're not both in the working mindset, you know?"

Taemin nodded. "I can understand that. It's a little like that with Preeti and Mr. Avi. Even if they both insist on calling me Master Choi even in downtime."

Marcus chuckled. "I can see that. Can't say I blame them."

"Well," Taemin said, "I'm glad you're not in the habit anymore."

Marcus looked at him, expression playful. "Me too. And? What about you? How did training go today?"

"Really well," Taemin said. "Brutal, but it always is. You always feel so accomplished after pushing that hard."

"Not too hard, though, right?" Marcus still looked playful, but it seemed like there was an undercurrent of real concern.

Taemin shook his head, hoping to dispel it. "Nothing I can't handle."

"Right, of course. How was the exhibition on Saturday?"

They chatted easily back and forth as they ate. Taemin was a little surprised at how hungry he ended up being, though he supposed he shouldn't have been. After all, he hadn't eaten a whole lot yesterday, and his breakfast had been pretty light, what with going to train in the morning. Between the two of them, they decimated the food.

"What time does filming start tomorrow?" Taemin asked as he went to wash the dishes. He had a dishwasher, but he mostly used it as a glorified drying rack. With only him eating—and, to be fair, sometimes forgetting to—it was rarely worth it to run the dishwasher. Marcus came up beside him to talk over the sound of water. He'd offered to help, which Taemin had immediately refused.

"Not sure when filming actually'll start, but my call time is nine. That's when I've got to be on set for hair and makeup. Billy's picking me up from my apartment around eight thirty."

"Are you looking forward to getting started?"

"Oh yeah, for sure. I've been reading the script—different versions of the script—for weeks now. I've talked to London, a lot of the rest of the cast, I'm getting choreography for stunts and fights—I'm ready to start putting it all together."

"Good, then. Sounds like it'll be a lot of fun. Hard work, but fun."

"That's about right." Marcus grinned. "It's a good life."

"I'm glad."

Two dishes and sets of cutlery cleaned up fast. Taemin set them aside to dry and then turned around fully, looking up at Marcus and—not hesitating before taking his hand to lead him into the living room. Marcus curled his fingers around Taemin's own and followed.

"Would you like to watch something?" Taemin asked, feeling—not nervous, but definitely butterflies, as they sat next to each other on the couch.

Marcus smiled. "Sure, that sounds good. What did you have in mind?"

Taemin laughed a little ruefully. "I was hoping you might be able to suggest something. You pretty much know my tastes."

"Okay, sure. Let me see what's playing right now."

Marcus picked an action movie that Taemin had never heard of, but one Marcus liked. ("I know the guy who plays the main character and the girl who plays his little sister. They've got a great dynamic onscreen.") They settled back to watch it, pressed against each other, Marcus's arm a warm weight across Taemin's shoulders.

The movie was interesting, but Taemin felt himself drifting as it went on. It was just peaceful. Being held by Marcus in the comfort of Taemin's living room. And he had to admit to being a little tired. Maybe… if he just closed his eyes….

MARCUS WASN'T completely sure when Taemin fell asleep, tucked up against him, but it was a bit of a thrill to be trusted so much. All he did was pull him a little closer and turn the sound down on the TV.

Taemin stirred just as the credits were starting to roll.

"Hey," Marcus murmured. "You awake?"

"Mm?" Taemin blinked sleepily up at him. God, he was cute. "I'm sorry. I didn't mean to fall asleep. It looks like I missed the movie." He sounded disappointed.

"It's okay," Marcus said. "We can always just watch it again. And I'm sure you needed the rest."

Taemin pulled away enough to roll out his neck, then immediately nuzzled back into Marcus. Marcus sighed happily and reached for his hand, stroking his thumb over the back of Taemin's knuckles. Taemin shifted to bring Marcus's hand up to kiss it, then turned more toward him.

Marcus met him for the kiss, arms coming to curl around Taemin's back and pull him closer, Taemin going easily, eagerly.

Soft, sleepy kisses turned heated, Marcus licking into Taemin's mouth before, at the vivid memory, he nipped his lower lip.

Taemin let out a soft gasp that only made Marcus desperate to hear it again. He moved to kiss underneath Taemin's jaw, then lower, pulling Taemin's T-shirt down to nose at his collarbone, and sucked there, reveling in Taemin's broken moan, the feel of his fingers flexing against Marcus's back. "Good?" he asked against Taemin's skin.

Taemin whimpered, then tugged on Marcus's shirt, pulling him back up to kiss him. Marcus was only too happy to oblige.

Kissing Taemin was dizzying, having him here in Marcus's arms, responding so beautifully. Marcus wanted more, more touches, more kisses, more sounds, everything Taemin was willing to give.

When they both paused for air, panting and staring into each other's eyes, Taemin smiled, this shy, bright little flash, before he reached forward, hand coming to rest just on Marcus's waist. His fingers dipped underneath Marcus's shirt before they stilled. "Okay?"

"Very, very okay," Marcus said, grinning. "I could just take it off."

Taemin's laugh was barely an exhale. "I would not say no."

Marcus's own laugh was a little louder as he pulled his shirt over his head and dropped it to the floor.

Taemin placed his hands on Marcus's shoulders, then stroked them down Marcus's chest, Marcus shuddering as he did so. He caught one of Taemin's hands and pressed his lips to his wrist, trailed a line of kisses up Taemin's arm as he moved Taemin back down against the couch cushions. When he reached the sleeve of Taemin's shirt, he tugged a little at the fabric with his teeth before he let go.

Taemin grinned up at him. "Was that a hint?"

Marcus smirked. "If you wanted it to be."

Taemin sat up—no hands, just an unassisted sit-up, and Marcus gave him just enough room to allow Taemin to pull his shirt over his head. Marcus immediately honed in on his collarbone again as Taemin clutched at him, breathing loud and ragged.

Marcus spent long minutes happily working on Taemin's jaw, neck, and collar. He was careful not to suck too hard, not where it would be visible, but the temptation was ridiculously strong. Especially considering how arousing Taemin's reactions were.

They were both hard now, moving against each other, until Taemin, after pulling Marcus up for another wet, messy kiss, put a hand on his shoulder. "Marcus?"

Marcus tried to catch his breath. "Yeah?"

Taemin licked his lips, now flushed and swollen. Marcus tracked his pink tongue before nudging him gently when Taemin didn't say anything. "Yeah?" he asked again. "What's up?"

"I—I know it's soon. But—"

Marcus stopped breathing. "But?" he prompted when Taemin paused.

Taemin bit his lip, then let out a breath. "I know it's soon," he said again. "So please don't feel pressured if you don't feel ready, but… I'd love to have you come to bed with me. If you wanted."

He wanted. He *absolutely* wanted. "Yes," Marcus breathed. "Yes, yeah, if—if you're sure—"

At that, Taemin smiled at him, face flushed, hair a mess, the most beautiful thing Marcus had ever seen. "Very, very sure." He moved fluidly off the couch to standing, then took Marcus's hand and tugged him to his feet. Marcus went, happy to go wherever Taemin wanted him, but even more so now.

TAEMIN LED him into his bedroom. It was bright and open, just like the rest of the apartment, with minimal furnishings: a bed, side tables and lamp, a wire-frame bookshelf filled with plants. Here, the walls weren't decorated, just a calm off-white, surrounding Taemin's dark blue bedspread.

The bed was neatly made, which was completely expected, but Taemin pulled the comforter down, so it was just the sheets, also a dark blue. Marcus watched dumbly as Taemin sat down on the bed and motioned him forward. “Come here?”

Throat dry, Marcus stepped closer, hovering in front of him. “I—can I—”

In answer, Taemin reached for his hand, tugging him forward as he scooted backward on the bed, to let Marcus climb up next to him. Now Marcus was the one to reach for Taemin, gently coaxing him onto his back. Taemin went easily, smiling up at him, and the only thought left in Marcus’s head after seeing that expression now was the intent to take Taemin completely apart.

One touch at a time.

He moved to blanket Taemin, catching his mouth again, thrilling as Taemin’s arms came to wrap around his back and pull him ever closer. He used one hand to brace above Taemin’s head so he didn’t completely crush him, trailing the other hand down until he could stroke his thumb over the top of Taemin’s hip, just where his shorts started. “Okay?”

“Yes,” Taemin managed between kisses, shifting. “Here, let me—”

“Can I?”

Taemin blinked up at him, startled, before he grinned. “Whatever you’d like.”

Marcus grinned back as his heart raced faster. “That’s giving me a lot of power.”

Taemin chuckled. Pinned underneath Marcus, splayed out and open. “I trust you.”

Marcus had to kiss him again, take his mouth even as his free hand trailed just a little lower, popped the button on Taemin’s shorts and unzipped, before he slid his hand inside.

Taemin bucked up underneath him at the touch, letting out a quiet moan that Marcus greedily swallowed before he started to kiss down Taemin’s chest, tongue circling a nipple and then sucking it into his mouth. This time the moan was louder, Marcus smiling against Taemin's skin before he moved to the other nipple, still stroking him inside his shorts. Taemin clutched at Marcus's shoulders before he pushed at him lightly. Marcus obligingly pulled back. "Too much?"

Taemin shook his head. Then he grinned up at Marcus, hooked his ankle around Marcus's own, and neatly flipped them over.

Marcus blinked up at him. "Okay," he said breathlessly. "Wow."

Taemin's fingers found the waistband of Marcus's own shorts. "May I?"

"Better idea, if you're okay with it," Marcus managed. "All clothes can go."

Taemin laughed, sounding just as breathless, before he got up and off Marcus. Marcus was disappointed for all of two seconds before Taemin shimmied out of his shorts and briefs. Then he took a moment to simply look at him.

Taemin shifted on the bed. "I'm hoping that expression means you see something you like." He sounded playful, but there might have been an undercurrent of worry there.

"You are the sexiest fucking thing I have ever seen," Marcus panted. *And I get to have this. I get to have you.*

"You're not so bad yourself." Taemin tugged at the hem of Marcus's shorts. "Off?"

Marcus wriggled out of his clothes and dropped them over the side of the bed, then kneeled back up to catch Taemin for another kiss.

They shifted until they were horizontal again, Taemin back on top, propped on Marcus's chest as they traded messy kisses, grinding against each other, movements getting desperate.

Marcus, well and truly overwhelmed, came first, curling up underneath Taemin, his groan punched out of him. He barely gave himself time to catch his breath, though, before he rolled them over, pressing down to feel every inch of skin as he curled a hand around Taemin.

When Taemin came, it was with a gasp, head thrown back, legs tightening around Marcus's own where they were tangled together.

He was so, so gorgeous.

Taemin adjusted them until they were lying on their sides facing each other as they both caught their breath. He leaned in to press a light kiss to Marcus's cheek, a quick, gentle thing, before he nuzzled into Marcus's chest. Marcus immediately brought his hands up to hold him.

"I like this," Taemin said quietly, after several long moments of peaceful silence. "Just having you here with me, like this."

"So do I," Marcus said.

WHEN TAEMIN blinked awake, the lighting in the room had changed, denoting the fact that it was now early evening. He shifted in Marcus's arms, and Marcus stirred next to him.

"Mm?"

And that was a sight, watching Marcus slowly open his eyes. And smile, sleepy but so bright. "Hey there."

Taemin couldn't help but smile back. "Hey. We ended up drifting, it looks like."

Marcus sat up and stretched. Taemin admired the lines of him. "Can't say I minded waking up to you."

"Same here," Taemin said. Because oh, he really hadn't.

Marcus reached out a hand to cup his cheek before leaning in to kiss him. When he pulled back, he looked rueful. "We should probably get cleaned up. If nothing else because it looks like it might be dinnertime. And even if we ordered in, I think the delivery people would appreciate if we wore clothes."

Taemin hadn't even thought about that, but he supposed Marcus was probably right. However, "I'm not sure how right you are, about them wanting you to be dressed."

Marcus grinned at him. "Yeah?"

"But I really would prefer having you all to myself."

A laugh. "Me too."

Taemin got up off the bed, rolling his shoulders as he stood up. "Would you like a shower?"

Marcus looked at him mischievously. "Do I get you in it with me?"

"If you feel like following me in," Taemin said playfully over his shoulder as he walked to the bathroom.

Both of them were used to quick showers, but now they took their time, washing each other instead of themselves and kissing under the spray. When they both finally did emerge, it was to pink cheeks and a cloud of steam.

They detoured back to Taemin's bedroom to grab their discarded bottoms, then headed out into the living room for their shirts. When Taemin went to put his on, Marcus waved a hand. "Wait," he said plaintively. "We haven't even ordered food yet. Can I get you shirtless for a little bit longer?"

Taemin laughed but obligingly folded his shirt and placed it on the arm of the couch. "Better?"

"Much," Marcus said with feeling. "What are you in the mood for?"

Taemin raised an eyebrow and tracked his eyes up and down Marcus's body, appreciating the fact that he, too, was still shirtless.

Marcus snickered. "Okay, point taken. But seriously, to eat?" He held up his phone.

"Are you sure you don't mind eating in again?"

"Not at all. I'd really rather be here with you. I much prefer your eyes on me, over the public's ones."

Taemin nodded in understanding. "Well, all right. Panera, maybe? Since we had Chinese food for lunch, I think I'd like something a little lighter."

"Yeah, that sounds great. Let's do that."

When their food arrived, they took it back to the couch instead of eating at the kitchen table, sitting side-by-side and talking about the week's plans.

"I can't believe you leave next Friday," Marcus said, when the trials came up.

"I know! I'm still not sure I'm ready, but I also am about as ready as I'll ever be, I think."

"You've been working really hard."

That was certainly true. Taemin nodded. "All to get better, though. I'm really looking forward to seeing how I do."

"I can't wait to hear all about it."

Chapter Eleven

ON MONDAY Marcus's movie went into full-on production mode, and his days were suddenly a lot busier, full of training, shooting, and more training. With Taemin's schedule too, they pretty much had no time to see each other except late at night, when they both were exhausted. They kept up a constant stream of texting throughout the day, though, which helped with the distance, and Taemin made a point each day to let Marcus know when he was about ready for bed so they could at least have a phone conversation to exchange good-nights.

The following Thursday, though, Marcus had ensured he didn't have to be on set until ten, which was also when Taemin went to volunteer. That meant that they had time to at least grab breakfast together. Playfully, Marcus had also offered that they go for a few minutes on the mat first. For a good luck send-off, even though he was going to be going over to Taemin's place that evening for a more personal goodbye.

Taemin had been delighted by the idea at the time. He still was, when he dragged himself out of bed Thursday morning, just also a little tired. He and Marcus had agreed on eight, to maximize their time both on the mat and then at breakfast. So another early morning, on top of the late night. Not that he wasn't used to those by now, after a steady stream of them for almost a month.

Since he was going to breakfast right after he and Marcus had their mat time, he didn't bother to eat anything before he headed over to Choi's, just made sure he had a bottle of his tea drink.

Marcus showed up a few minutes after Taemin turned on the lights. "Good timing," Taemin said as Marcus stepped out of his shoes, bowed onto the mat, and then came over to kiss Taemin good morning.

Marcus quirked his lips. "Rule of the set. Fifteen minutes early is on time. Get there on time and you're late."

"That's a good rule."

"Yeah, I think so too. So? You ready to wipe the floor with me?"

Taemin rolled his eyes. "We'll go a few rounds and have some fun."

"Sounds good to me."

They geared up and started their own warm-ups and stretches. Taemin went over to one of the bags to get an extended leg stretch. He breathed into it and then dropped his leg carefully. Wobbled a little before he went to stretch the other one. He still felt sort of tired.

Nothing he couldn't handle, though.

"I'm about ready," Marcus said several minutes later.

"Great." Taemin smiled, turning to him. "Let's get started!"

They met in the middle of the mat, bowed to each other, and started bounding, circling each other to gauge.

Taemin moved first, striking out with a quick roundhouse that wasn't even for points—just to get the match moving. Marcus blocked, and that was all they needed to really begin the fight.

Taemin had to blink spots out of his eyes after his first spin-kick, refinding his equilibrium in a way he usually didn't have to. It was just in time that he brought up a hand to block Marcus's next movement: a brutally powerful sidekick. He staggered with the force of it, and—that wasn't *right.* He'd taken way harder hits without feeling them like this.

He was just tired. And, okay, maybe he should have eaten something before stepping into the ring so early after too little sleep, but—

He whipped around to score on Marcus's head with a jump-spinning hook kick, the fast movement dizzying in a way it never was—

His legs collapsed underneath him, and he barely caught himself on his hands and knees.

"Taemin!"

"I'm fine, I—" He tried to stand and fell right back down onto the floor, the headrush overpowering. "I—" He put one hand to his temple and just tried to breathe, the spots blinking back into his vision.

He felt more than saw Marcus crouching down next to him and place a supporting arm on his back, guiding him to sit more fully. "Let me get you some water," Marcus said quickly, standing and nearly running to the side of the mat, where they'd left their water bottles. He was back moments later, shoving the bottle into Taemin's hands. "Drink, okay?"

Taemin nodded, then immediately stilled, trying to calm the sudden headache. He unscrewed the bottle's cap and drank in long pulls, gasping when he was finished. "Sorry about that," he said, embarrassed. "I'm good to go now."

Marcus frowned. "What are you talking about?"

Taemin moved to stand, bracing his hands on his knees for a moment before standing fully. "Sparring. Let's go again." He smiled ruefully. "I think you won the last round."

"Wha—no." Marcus looked a mixture of baffled and concerned. "Of course not. We're done for the day. You need to rest."

Taemin huffed. "I'm perfectly all right." He'd had a few of those dizzy spells lately. They passed quickly enough. "If I can't push through, how do you think I'll do for the actual trials?"

Marcus looked at him, wide-eyed. "Taemin, you—you can't compete like this."

Taemin frowned, starting to feel irritable. That wasn't a light accusation. "Stop making this out to be such a big deal. I'm fine."

"You just collapsed," Marcus said. He sounded like he was struggling to keep his voice even. "You're not taking care of yourself. That's no way to go into a major competition."

"I have been doing this for longer than you have been alive," Taemin said, scowling. "As I have said on *multiple occasions*, I know how to handle myself."

"Do you? Have you gone this hard for this long before?"

"Marcus—"

"You're going to seriously get hurt if you step into a ring like this. You've pushed yourself too much."

"I'll thank you not to count on me failing," Taemin said hotly. "I don't leave until tomorrow, and the matches aren't until the day after. That's plenty of time to rest and recover."

"That's barely two days. *You* were the one who taught me to give it at least three days' rest before a major competition!"

"That is enough," Taemin said through gritted teeth. "I am sick of being told what I can and can't do. I am not a child. I have been training for these trials for months. Yes? I have been training for months. I know what I'm doing."

Marcus stepped forward. "Taemin, come on. You've got to see what you're doing to yourself. If you'd just listen to me—"

Taemin didn't want to listen. His head hurt, he felt shaky, and he was already embarrassed for showing that sort of weakness in the first place. And Marcus was going on about how he wasn't fit to do something he'd been training all his life for? He didn't know what he was talking about. Taemin's father would have already started the next round. "You've barely been back in my life a month. You have no right to talk."

Marcus looked stricken. "Taemin, please—"

Marcus had *no right* to look like that. Not when he was telling Taemin that he wasn't good enough. "You can see yourself out," Taemin said, turning and walking quickly into his office. He wanted distance and to breathe and to sit down, and his head was pounding.

Minutes later, he distantly heard the jingle of the front door open and close.

Taemin braced himself against his desk, furious. At himself, at Marcus, at how awful he felt.

His plane left in twenty-four hours and all he wanted to do was crawl back into bed.

MARCUS LEFT the dojang feeling like his head was stuffed full of cotton wool. He was equal parts upset and terrified. Upset because a fight with Taemin had been the last thing he'd wanted, especially before something so big, and Marcus was only concerned for him. For how hard he was pushing himself, for how clearly that was taking a toll on his body.

And terrified, because if Taemin stepped into a ring the way he was now, he could get seriously hurt. A dizzy spell or faltered step at the wrong moment, at the speed and intensity competitive athletes moved—god, the possibility of injury was high even when you were *on* your game.

And the worst part was that he couldn't do anything. He'd tried to say his piece and Taemin had gotten upset, and… and Marcus couldn't blame him for that. If someone had told *him* that he was unfit for a part he'd been prepping for for ages….

He sat in his car, head in his hands. "Fuck," he groaned. Now what?

He could go back inside, apologize, but even if Taemin was willing to listen to it—and Marcus doubted that; he'd made him *upset*—that wouldn't change anything. He still thought Taemin shouldn't fly out tomorrow morning.

They were going to have a nice night together. Say goodbye and celebrate Taemin's chances.

His phone beeped. Billy. *I'm really sorry. London wanted to switch a shot sequence around. Can you get over here and to makeup? Reply needed asap.*

I'll be right there, Marcus typed, feeling lost. He had work to do at least. Concentrate on that for now. Give Taemin time to cool down. Marcus would apologize to him in person when he got off work. And they could figure the rest out then.

Because he'd been planning to eat with Taemin—and that obviously hadn't happened, he thought bitterly—he stopped to grab something from a Dunkin' Donuts to eat on the way over. Billy met him onsite, whisking him away to makeup.

"I'm really sorry," Billy said after a few moments of silence. "You know the last thing I wanted to do was interrupt."

"There was nothing to interrupt," Marcus said, feeling tired. "I was about leaving when you texted me anyway."

Billy frowned. “What? Why? I thought you were going to have a morning together?”

“So did I.”

“Okay? So? What the hell.”

“Remember how we talked about him not, uh, being the best at taking care of himself?”

“Sure?”

“He collapsed during our sparring sessions this morning.”

“Oh my god, is he okay?”

“He’d like to think he is,” Marcus said bitterly.

“O… kay. So what does that mean?”

Marcus told Billy about what happened. What he said, and Taemin’s response. “—and now I don’t know what to do. I can’t say anything, because it’ll just upset him, but I can’t keep quiet either. He’s really hurting himself. And the idea of him stepping onto a mat—”

“No, yeah, fuck. I get it.”

“Yeah,” Marcus said miserably.

“You said that he brought up how long you’ve been together,” Billy said hesitantly. “Is there someone who’s maybe known him for longer? That he might listen to?”

Marcus immediately thought of Preeti and Mr. Avi. But Preeti might be too young to make Taemin really pay attention. He’d brushed her off before, and Marcus could easily see him doing so again. So Mr. Avi, maybe? At least he could try.

He didn’t have Mr. Avi’s number to ask, but he figured Preeti did. Once he’d been given the go-ahead from makeup, he sent her a quick text while he and Billy headed over to set.

When he had a moment to check his phone, he’d gotten a response. *Sure, I can give it to you. But why?*

I need someone who might be able to talk sense into Taemin.

Oh no, that doesn’t sound good. What happened?

Remember when you told me the story about him fainting after nationals?

Yeah…?

That.

WHAT. When??

This morning, Marcus replied. *We were having a friendly match and he collapsed. Tried to tell me everything was fine and that we should pick right back up where we left off.*

Asdfghjkl Master Choi NO. Yeah, okay, I'll text Mr. Avi. I can give you his number too.

Thank you.

Of course. Are you coming by Choi's tonight?

Absolutely. I want to talk to him in person again before he leaves.

I can imagine. Okay, see you then. And I'll update you if I learn anything before then.

Thanks, Marcus sent back with feeling.

TAEMIN'S DARK mood colored his whole morning, even though he tried his best not to let it. Especially during his volunteer time. When he was done with the hospital, though, he went straight home. Rattled around in his apartment, unable to keep from feeling annoyed, and then just gave up and crawled under his covers; his headache still hadn't abated.

He pulled himself up a couple hours later, feeling groggy and not at all well rested. Washing his face helped some. He also went to his kitchen to get something to eat. He hadn't felt like it after Marcus had left—and then had gone to the hospital and….

And now it was almost three o'clock.

Was this really the first time he'd eaten today?

The thought struck him hard. That after having that fun little episode on the mat where his body had obviously needed fuel, he just… hadn't.

It had been a common pattern these last few months, since he'd added in his extra training. Forgetting to eat, not having enough time to sleep, working so hard because he only had so much time in a day, and then, of course, making time for Marcus….

It was little food, littler sleep, and a lot of stress he was putting on his body aside from that.

Marcus had only been concerned. And—and obviously worried.

And Taemin had yelled at him.

He had to apologize. He went to grab his phone, then paused. Marcus was at work. Taemin wasn't going to disturb him with a phone call, and it didn't feel right to just text him. But what else could he do?

As he unlocked his phone, he was startled to find text messages from both Mr. Avi and Preeti.

He opened Mr. Avi's first. *Don't come to class today. You need to rest up for your flight tomorrow, and the competition. Preeti and I can hold down the fort.*

And Preeti's, *MASTER CHOI IF YOU DON'T EAT LUNCH AND TAKE A NAP I WILL FLY TO KOREA TO TELL GRANDMASTER CHOI ON YOU*

Taemin couldn't help but laugh softly. They cared about him. That's all it was. Good intentions and… not unnecessary ones, considering what he'd been doing to himself without even thinking about it.

He opened a group chat and wrote a message to both of them. *I plan to come to class today, if only to say goodbye to everyone before I fly out tomorrow. But I'll take it easy, I promise. I trust you both to lead classes. I have plenty to do in my office anyway.*

He sent off the message and then got started on his meal. His phone buzzed a few minutes later. Preeti had sent him several exclamation marks and thumbs-up emojis. Mr. Avi had written, *Fine, but you better actually take it easy, or I'm making you go home.*

Mutiny, he sent back, before concentrating on his food.

When he finished, he washed his dishes and eventually moved to his couch, giving himself more time to work through his thoughts.

He did want to apologize to Marcus. Taemin had been frustrated with himself, at his body betraying him, and he'd taken it out on Marcus, who hadn't deserved it.

But Taemin's knee-jerk reaction to apologize aside, Marcus hadn't been entirely in the right either. Especially with telling Taemin that he wasn't competition-ready. All right, so Taemin knew he was a little fatigued and could stand a *real* few good nights of sleep, as well as some more regularly scheduled meals. But telling him he shouldn't go compete?

At least Preeti and Mr. Avi understood. They were also pushing for him to rest—but with the intention of sending him to the trials in top form. They knew how important this was to him. How much he wanted to make a good showing, especially since he probably wouldn't be doing this again. At least not something of this caliber. The academy and his other activities simply took too much of his time for him to fly all over the country to compete. Of course, it was true that competing in the Olympics would be a great way to showcase his own skills in taekwondo—and help to uphold the Choi name. And he would be the first to admit how badly he wanted to compete for his own personal satisfaction too.

But he was also tired.

He and Marcus had been very wrapped up in each other these last few weeks. Talking was easy; the company was comforting; the intimacy was wonderful. However it had also been a lot very quickly. And Taemin had something else he needed to focus on right now.

Decision made, he unlocked his phone to send Marcus a text.

MARCUS HAD two text messages waiting for him when he got a break in filming to check his phone. One was from Preeti: a screenshotted image of a message Taemin had sent to her about promising to take it easy that evening.

And another from Taemin. *I'm sorry*, it said. *I understand why you said what you did. I apologize for my own behavior. But I also think this might be a good time to take a step back, for a little while. I need to keep my head in the game right now. Maybe we can talk more when I get back?*

Marcus stared at the message. The "so I don't want to see you" wasn't written out, but it glared a bright red all the same.

He swallowed. What else could he say? *Of course. I understand. I'm sorry too. Good luck out there. I'll be rooting for you.*

He received a *thank you* a few minutes later. And nothing else.

"You look like someone shot your dog, man," Leo said, clapping him on the shoulder. "The scene's not going that bad, is it?"

Marcus shook his head. "Scene's going fine," he said, trying to sound light. "It's a good energy out there."

"Okay," Leo said slowly. "And something's really wrong, huh? What's going on?"

"Nothing. Really." He glanced down at his phone. "Just, uh, just taking a step back, it looks like."

Leo frowned in confusion. "Looks like?"

Marcus sighed. "Taemin and I sort of had a fight this morning. He just apologized to me about it. But, uh, also said that maybe we should wait to see each other again until he gets back from the trials."

"The Olympic trials, right?"

"Yeah."

"And he… doesn't want to see you before he leaves?"

"Yeah," Marcus said again, quietly.

"*Why?*"

"I don't know. I don't know. I just hope I haven't fucked things up."

"Don't think like that," Leo said quickly. "He says he wants to see you again, just not right now. That's something. It sounds like maybe he's got some of his own shit to deal with and he wants some time for that. I mean, the Olympics is a big deal."

"Right," Marcus said. "Yeah."

"It'll be okay," Leo assured him. "He apologized to you. That's, you know, that's important."

Marcus nodded.

"And I mean, look, you saw him mad today, right?"

"Um, right."

Leo looked at him. "But you still think he hung the moon."

It wasn't a question, because it didn't need to be. "Yeah."

"Right," Leo said. "You hold on to something like that."

"Only if he wants to be held, though," Marcus said miserably.

"Yeah," Leo said after a moment. "Okay, I get that. Yeah." He cleared his throat. "But I really don't think you need to worry. Just, you know, wait 'til he comes back. Have a conversation. At least it sounds like he wants to have one."

"Right." It sounded like Taemin did want to talk, just not right now. And he did have something incredibly important at the forefront of his mind. It made sense.

Didn't make it suck any less, but it made sense.

Chapter Twelve

WHEN TAEMIN arrived at his hotel room, his first order of business was to go out for a meal. He was going to try to make it a priority to actually follow a schedule for when he ate. Obviously he didn't want to eat too close to full-on training, but he spent his time on the plane reading some articles—ironically, that Preeti had sent him but he'd never gotten around to—about how to plan out eating for maximum performance, especially with carb and protein cycling. So a full meal an hour or two before a training session, something light about thirty minutes before, and then something to refuel after. It was an awful lot to keep in mind, especially being so unused to paying attention to food, but he was going to put in the effort to try.

Second order of business was to settle in for a nap. One, he could digest while unconscious, and two, it would help get his energy up again. He was going to go full rest-day, with the exception of stretching. Being in top form was important. He was good. He knew he was good. So he had to show that.

When he woke up, he went to take a long walk, just to be outside and get out of his hotel room, as well as to help pass the time. After returning to the hotel, he had work to do on his laptop until he needed to get dinner. He did his best to keep occupied, but… every so often he reached for his phone. Scrolled through his messages until he got to the conversation with Marcus. *Good luck out there. I'll be rooting for you.*

Every time he sighed and set his phone back down. He missed Marcus. He'd only had him back in his life for a few weeks, but he'd already become someone to miss. Maybe he'd been wrong to leave without seeing him. But at the same time, he felt like he'd be stronger for this. He was doing something on his own, without Marcus, even with how important he'd become, and mountains weren't moving.

Next time he'd like to share the experience with him, though.

Time passed like syrup until it was time for him to go to bed, even with him turning in early. He got under the covers and closed his eyes to meditate. Try to calm his mind and his heart to prepare for tomorrow.

He wasn't sure when he dropped off to sleep, but when he woke up with his alarm, it was to barely contained excitement. It was here. What he'd been working toward for months. It was finally *here*.

He'd gotten up early specifically so he could get breakfast and give it time to metabolize before he went to the gym where the trials were being held. After breakfast he took a shower, did a simple warm-up and stretches (he'd *really* warm up at the gym), and spent some time on his phone, smiling at all the messages and posts on the academy's Facebook wishing him good luck.

Good luck out there. I'll be rooting for you.

Soon enough it was time to head out. He grabbed up his duffel bag and made his way over to the gym.

It was even more exciting once he was there, looking at the mat and all the other competitors warming up and otherwise getting ready.

"Master Choi! Hey, glad to see you made it!"

"Master Adams," Taemin said, delighted, going to shake his hand. Master Adams pulled him into an embrace, slapping him on the back. "Good to see you again."

"Same, same. Competition's going to be given a real run for its money, with you here."

"I could say the same about you." Taemin grinned. Master Adams was an old friend, years of history between them as they'd moved through taekwondo circles. He was in a different weight class than Taemin, so they'd never had an "official" competitive match, though they'd had plenty just for fun. Master Adams had medaled bronze four years ago. "Going for the gold this time?"

"Absolutely. Just gotta get there first."

They made small talk, them and several other masters who came up to say hello and catch up. A big competition like this was pretty much a black-belt convention. Everyone was looking forward to seeing what they could do and how far they could go.

Soon enough, though, it was time to get back into it. They all separated to warm up and stretch, and then they were divided up by weight class and taken to different parts of the huge mat to begin the elimination rounds.

"PICTURE IS up! Everyone settle, please. This is picture. Camera ready?"

"Ready!"

"Sound ready?"

"Ready!"

"London, ready?"

"Ready."

"Okay! Boom in, slate in. Roll sound."

"Speed!"

"Scene one hundred twenty-nine, fight two, take six."

"Roll camera!"

"Speed!"

"Marker."

"Action," London said, focusing in on the off-camera screen.

"Come on, kid," Marcus said, holding a hand out to Hailey. "It's been a long day, huh? Let's get back to the ship."

Hailey shook her head, looking mutinous. "I'm not going. They'll just keep following you. I can hide out on my own."

Marcus sighed. "Do you really want to do this now?"

"I'm not going!" Then her eyes widened, and Marcus turned to follow what she was looking at.

"Cut! Set for stunt fight!"

Marcus and Hailey froze while the stuntmen got into their positions.

"Ready?"

"Speed."

"Marker."

"Action!"

Marcus waited for the thumbs-up from Leo, just off to the side, and then he moved, twisting away from the punch being thrown at his head. Hailey screamed as she was picked up, kicking and struggling, while Marcus fought to get at her. They went through the whole action sequence of Marcus being subdued while Hailey was whisked away. "And cut!"

Marcus took the hand up off the ground and nodded to Daniel, who saluted.

"Re-set! Angle on camera three. Makeup?"

Hailey and Marcus got back into their positions, the stuntmen also stepping into place. Natasha, from makeup, padded away the sweat on Marcus's forehead—it was fucking *hot* in his full wardrobe—and then went to smooth down Hailey's hair. London looked them both over and nodded. "Good. Okay people, let's do it again!"

It was intensive work that took up Marcus's energy and attention, and he was grateful that he had it today to pass the time and keep him busy and keep him from checking his phone every five minutes to see if Taemin had sent him an update.

He'd gotten a text from Taemin yesterday saying that he'd landed safely but no word since then. Taemin really had meant it when he said he was going dark. Marcus had agonized over whether to send him another good luck text that morning but had decided against it in the end. Since Taemin wanted to do this himself, then Marcus would let him. He could show Taemin that he *did* respect him and his choices.

No matter what happened with the trials, Marcus would be there for Taemin to come back to. Ready to talk, ready to listen, and willing to do what he could to make things work for the both of them.

TAEMIN TOOK out his mouth guard and grabbed up his water bottle, emptying a good half of it in one go. Seven matches down. Seven wins. He was doing his best and so far, it had been good enough.

His stamina wasn't deserting him either, which pleased him to no end. Thursday had really worried him, but after a good night's sleep Thursday and Friday evening, on top of actually remembering to eat at reasonable times… he was holding his own.

Seven matches down, seven wins, eight to go.

He used his break to observe some of the other competitors as they participated in their own rounds. Ate half an energy bar and drank some more water. Spent some time taking several deep breaths to recenter himself.

When he was called back up, he stood and pulled his helmet back on, put his mouth guard back in. Stepped to the middle of the mat in front of the referee. Bowed when he was instructed to, and then the match was off.

The pace was brutal, fantastic just like all the other matches had been. He kept his arms up and went for as many points as fast as he could. That had been his strategy all along—get in, go fast, *score.*

The match was called, points to him. Another round done, another round won.

Taemin breathed out. He was getting closer.

Another match, points to him.

Closer.

Time stopped but for the match beginnings and endings, and his focus narrowed down to speed and movement, blocks and attacks. Tenth round, eleventh, twelfth—

Thirteenth round and he was up against a man on the larger end of the weight class. With him being on the lower end, that meant a shift in balance; he probably had more speed, his opponent probably had more power. Hopefully it would even out and Taemin would be able to take an advantage.

They bowed in, the referee signaled them to start, and his opponent immediately struck out with a kick so fast the leg on his dobok snapped. Taemin just managed to move out of the way, but the speed *and* power of his opponent was clear. He would manage a point, his opponent got two, three to Taemin, one to the competition.

At time for round two, they were tied. Reset for the third round, Sijak. They both went in for a kick at the same time, colliding and pushing each other back. Taemin recovered into a spin, aiming for the head, and his opponent brought his arm to block as he twisted away.

It was the wrong set of movements for both of them at exactly the wrong time, and his opponent's elbow collided at full-force with Taemin's shin. Taemin hissed in pain but recovered, setting his leg back onto the ground.

"*Gamjeom*!" the referee cried, throwing up a hand to stop the match.

Panting, Taemin froze, grateful for the short break; his leg was on fire.

The referee came up to determine if Taemin had been match-stoppingly injured. Taemin quickly assured him he was fine, and after some conferring, it was decided the match would continue.

With his opponent's penalty and only fifteen seconds left, Taemin played defensively until the match was called. Points to him. He'd won another round.

It was an effort not to limp off the mat as he was given his breather, but he pushed through the pain. Two more matches. He could absolutely take on two more matches.

"Sorry," his opponent said, coming up to him, clearly upset. He had a thick Russian accent. "So sorry. You step, I move wrong. Not mean to hit so hard that way."

"I know," Taemin assured him. "It's okay."

"Your moves very good," the man said. He held out a hand. "Sasha Petrov."

"Taemin Choi," Taemin said, shaking it. "Thank you."

"How long you train?"

"Thirty-four years, if you count childhood."

Sasha shook his head, grinning now. "Always should count. They make us work very hard."

"How long have you been practicing?"

"Nineteen years. I'm start when I'm seven."

They chatted a little longer in between sips of water, Taemin resting most of his weight on his right leg. He'd been lucky in that, at least. His right leg was stronger, his left more flexible, so most of his power needed to come from the right. That his dominant leg was still in good shape meant he had a much higher chance of moving forward.

"Your turn again," Sasha said, nodding at the ring when Taemin was called back. "Good luck. I'm hoping for you to win."

"Thank you," Taemin said before putting his helmet back on, mouth guard back in.

It wasn't too bad, walking to the ring now that he'd gotten a bit of rest. It was probably mostly shock, he thought, that had made his shin hurt the way it had at time of impact. Now things, okay, did still hurt, but he knew he'd be able to fight through. He stood in front of the referee and bowed to his new opponent.

"Sijak!"

Go hard, go fast, go strong. Breathe and think of *nothing else*. Pain had no business here. Taemin was going to fight and score and *win*—

First round to him.

Again.

Second round to his opponent.

Again.

Third round—

Taemin squeezed his eyes shut when the match was called. Points to him. He'd done it.

One more match.

MARCUS CHECKED his phone. Still nothing. It was about two o'clock, and he had been given a break while lighting and rigging worked on some set stuff. He used the time to drink and eat something, just to fuel his body. He really hadn't been kidding when he'd told Preeti about how much he had to eat to sustain himself.

Sometimes that even meant eating when he didn't feel like it or particularly want to.

And that was just getting him to think about Taemin yet again. How he was *doing*. How the competition was going of course, but how he was doing. Marcus couldn't get the image of Taemin falling to his knees out of his mind. He worried. Of course he worried. He wanted to check in, but he needed to give Taemin his space, and Taemin wouldn't have his phone on him anyway. So that didn't even matter. He'd talk to Marcus when he was ready. If he wanted to.

Marcus was rooting for him, but he hoped that if Taemin did make it, he'd try to still take a step back. Not run himself so hard into the ground. Surely he'd understand that to be in top form, there was only so far you could push your body before it became a detriment.

THE FOURTEENTH round had been a hard-won battle. Even if Taemin wasn't putting most of his weight on his left leg, it was still his main striking leg, not to mention he used it to bound, to circle, when he changed things up to strike with his right.

He hurt. He couldn't deny that he hurt. Fighting with the injury had only exacerbated it.

But he could do it. He could do one more.

However, first he had to go through the medical check. At the beginning of the trials, everyone competing had to undergo a medical check to make sure they were fit to participate. For the last round, there was another one for the two competitors, to determine that they were still good to go.

When the doctor came over to Taemin, he went straight for Taemin's left leg and prompted Taemin to pull up his dobok. He did so, wincing even at that small movement and then more so when he saw his leg.

A bruise the size of a fist already started to color the skin, a dark, angry purple. It… it looked pretty bad. The doctor felt around it carefully, Taemin hissing in pain, and then moved on, checking the rest of Taemin over.

When the check was complete, the doctor told Taemin to wait and then went to talk to the committee.

After several minutes of conferring, one of the judges came over.

"Doctor Mason says that you've probably bruised the bone, if not splintered it," he said. "You have two options. You could compete and possibly break your leg, or you can take a medical bye that will allow you to recompete at the next trials in four years."

Taemin took a shaky breath. That wasn't much of a choice. "The injury is that bad?"

The judge nodded. "Doctor Mason strongly suggests you take the bye."

Taemin's mind whirled. To give up now was almost unthinkable. He had to at least try, didn't he? He was skilled. And he was so close. He couldn't go home having just *given up*. What would he tell his school? They were all rooting for him. Expecting him to go all the way. What would he say about getting so far and then deciding he'd had enough?

But… what would he tell his students, who trusted him and looked up to him and saw him as a role model, if he pushed too hard and got seriously hurt as a result?

What would he say to them then?

What sort of example was he setting to be pushing himself so hard and brushing off the concerns of those he cared about? To even *consider* unnecessarily doing something that could result in a broken bone? If Jamal or Roshen, or even Preeti, had been doing to themselves what he had been doing to his own body….

Besides, if he did end up injuring himself that badly, he'd be useless. Forget competing at the games—he wouldn't be able to teach. And that… that was really the most important thing, wasn't it? Not bringing home medals to display at his school, but being able to run it the way he believed it should be run.

A bye was not what he wanted, but it still gave him a chance in four years. And he could take it knowing he had done his best. He'd competed in good form and gotten as far as the final match. He'd done well. Even if this wasn't how he wanted things to end.

What choice did he have, in the end?

He'd done well.

Taemin bowed his head. "I'll take the bye."

The judge nodded. "Let me speak to the rest of the committee."

Fifteen minutes later, and Taemin was on his way to urgent care. He had planned to stay after the fights were all over and go out with the other masters, but part of him couldn't summon up the strength to. Instead he said his goodbyes, traded contact information with the people he'd met anew (included Sasha, who had been stricken at the news), and went where Doctor Mason suggested.

An x-ray later and he had his leg tightly wrapped with instructions to do the minimum on it for at least a week, and no heavy exercise or lifting for at least three. Follow up with the doctor after. So Taemin went back to his hotel feeling pretty miserable.

He decided against letting anyone know. He was flying out that night anyway, and so would be back in Michigan before Sunday. He'd done that on purpose; the less time away, the better. And he had cleared his whole Sunday to make sure he really had time to recuperate.

He'd certainly need the time now, he thought, with a touch of bitterness.

The other thought was how much he wanted to see Marcus and apologize and be told that things would be okay.

MARCUS GOT a text from Taemin at about nine thirty that night.

Home, it said. *I hope you're doing well.*

Marcus swallowed. *Can I ask how things went? Is that okay?*

Are you free to talk right now?

Yeah, Marcus replied immediately. *Yeah, of course.*

His phone rang. Marcus fumbled to accept the call. "Hi," he said quietly.

"Hello," Taemin said. He sounded tired.

"How… how did it go?"

"Very well. I made to the last round."

"Oh! Oh wow, that's—that's great. I… was it the last round?"

"No," Taemin said. "I didn't compete. I got a medical bye."

Marcus's heart leapt into his throat. "What happened?"

There was a heavy sigh. "I did very well," Taemin said again. "There was a mishap in the thirteenth round. I was able to win the fourteenth as well, but that put too much stress on the injury. I was told I could fight and break my leg or that I could take the bye and compete again in four years."

Break his leg? That was *terrifying.* "Wow I… I'm so sorry."

"It's all right. I…." A pause then, so long it made Marcus ache. "I did what I set out to do. I competed. I got as far as I did. I just…."

"Could I come over?" Marcus asked. "If you want me to. If—if you maybe would like someone around. If you don't, then—then of course, but I don't know, maybe? I just—if you want me to. I'm here."

"It's okay. It's late. You don't have to."

"I want to," Marcus said in a rush, already going to put on his shoes. "Please, I—if it would help, please let me." *Please let me be there for you. And please let me see you again.*

"Then I'd like that," Taemin said after a moment. "Thank you."

Marcus grabbed his keys and wallet and hurried to his car, making the drive in less time than he should have. But no one pulled him over, and then he was going up the stairs to Taemin's floor and knocking on his door, and nothing mattered except making sure Taemin was all right.

Taemin was quiet as he let Marcus into his apartment. He had a pronounced limp as Marcus led him over to the couch and sat down with him, not touching him past holding his hand, waiting to see what Taemin wanted to do.

They sat in silence for a long time before Taemin opened his mouth. "I worked so hard." The words were quiet. "I worked so hard and I got *so far*. I did so well. I was going to do it. I knew I was."

Marcus had no doubt about that. "I know."

"But—but the idea of doing it again in four years… of pushing that much and being so tired and stretched so thin…. That's so daunting. I—I don't know if I could do it again."

Marcus swallowed. "I'm sorry."

Taemin shook his head. "I have so many other things in my life. It's okay. I keep… trying to tell myself that. I only have so much time. I want to make sure I use it the way I want to."

"Yeah." Marcus nodded. "Yeah, of course."

Taemin went quiet, looking pensive. "I think I'm going to go to bed," he said after several minutes. "Would… would you stay with me?"

"Of course." Not even a question. "Of course. Come on."

It was Marcus who tugged Taemin to his feet and led him into the bedroom. They undressed in silence, and then Taemin climbed into bed, holding up the covers for Marcus to slide in next to him.

Taemin turned into him then, pressed his face into the crook of Marcus's neck and shoulder. Marcus brought his arms to hold him, stroking one hand through his hair.

That was how they drifted off.

TAEMIN WOKE up warm, Marcus's arm draped across him. They'd moved in their sleep so that they were back to chest. Marcus curled around him. It was a very pleasant way to wake up. It—it would be nice to get that a little more often. With, perhaps, less of an awful reason leading to it.

He took a deep breath and gingerly sat up, moving away from Marcus, who slept on. Taemin took a moment just to look at his sleeping face. He was so, so lucky to have Marcus in his life. And he was going to talk to him about how much he wanted things to work. Being away from him had made him realize how much he *missed*. Not even the distance, but the fact that they hadn't talked through it.

He still wanted to discuss the fight. Why he'd reacted the way he had. What Marcus had said that—that wasn't okay. But he knew already that it was just a little bump, easy to overcome.

Walking the short distance to the bathroom was still painful, and the first thing he did was down a painkiller before he went to brush his teeth and take a quick shower. When he emerged from the bathroom about ten minutes later, it was to see Marcus sitting up, covers pooling around his waist. The morning sun almost made him glow.

He was so beautiful.

"Good morning," Taemin said, limping over to the bed so he could rewrap his leg.

"Hey," Marcus said sleepily. He leaned forward to press a kiss to Taemin's temple. "Morning."

"Thank you for staying with me."

"There wasn't anything I wanted to do more."

It made Taemin's breath catch. "Do you have to work today?"

Marcus shook his head. "I filmed yesterday, so I'm off today. Back to the grind on Monday. You?"

"I don't have anything to do today. Except contact people about what I can and can't do for the week."

"Oh. I'm sorry."

Taemin shook his head. "I'll get past it. Right now all I want to do is recover."

"What happened at the trials? You, um, you didn't really go into detail last night."

Taemin stood to hobble over to his closet. "An unfortunate turn of events had my opponent's elbow meet my shin," he said as he pulled on his clothes. He had to prop himself against the wall and move very carefully to pull on his bottoms. "It bruised the bone. But nothing cracked, so I count myself lucky."

"Fuck," Marcus said. "I'm so sorry. But you're okay? You—crutches?"

"I didn't want them," Taemin said. "I felt they'd inhibit more than help. I should be okay as long as I take it easy."

"Take it easy, huh?"

Taemin sighed. "I know. I'm going to do my best. I'd like to talk to you about it some more too."

"Okay," Marcus said easily. "Why don't I get ready and then we can go out for breakfast?"

"Okay."

Taemin found Marcus a toothbrush to use, and then Marcus took his clothes into the bathroom to change back into after his shower. It was only a few minutes later that he emerged to find Taemin sitting on his couch and staring at his phone.

"Everything okay?" Marcus asked.

Taemin shrugged. "I haven't told Preeti or Mr. Avi yet. I want to. I'm just not sure how. I don't want to paint what happened in a negative light. I went and, in a way, I won. I just… also didn't."

"You'll figure it out," Marcus said. "Maybe over breakfast? Do you have a place you'd like to go?"

"I'd kind of like to go to the Pancake House," Taemin admitted.

Marcus smiled. "That's a good plan. Let's do that."

MARCUS DROVE them to the Original Pancake House. Because it was Sunday there was a bit of a line, but at least neither of them had anywhere to be. Taemin leaned against him to take more weight off his leg, Marcus's arm curled around his shoulder.

On Marcus's end, he was wearing a ballcap pulled low over his eyes and just hoped no one noticed him.

Twenty minutes later they were seated in a booth and had ordered, waiting for their food.

"So," Taemin said after a moment.

"So," Marcus agreed.

"I'm sorry again. About how I acted on Thursday. How I spoke to you. What-what I said. I know it really hasn't been that long but I—I value your opinion. And I know you were just concerned."

"I'm sorry too," Marcus rushed to say. "You were working so hard and I was so worried, but I never should have said that you shouldn't compete. I just—I just worried, and you had scared me. You know your own limits. It's not my place to try to police you."

Taemin shook his head. "No, you… you were right. About some of it. Preeti and Mr. Avi have been saying the same things for years. I *do* often have trouble slowing down enough to realize that I need to stop. I think I just became so focused on winning and making a good showing, doing what I could to prepare, that I got a little lost."

Marcus nodded.

"I'll try to pay attention to myself more. And—" Taemin sighed. "—and if I want to make time for certain things, that might mean that some other things might need to be compromised on."

"Yeah?"

"For instance, if I want to see you as much as I can. Which I do! But that might not be realistic sometimes."

"Like trying to squeeze in a few hours in between a day's worth of classes and an evening exhibition?" Marcus asked wryly.

"Like planning my time a little bit better, so that I have some more wiggle room," Taemin allowed. "Compromising on how often I commit to things like my own tournaments and travel, if I do at all." His father's legacy aside, Taemin had enjoyed getting back into the competitive circuit. But it required so much of him. He could make those choices. He would.

"Hey," Marcus said gently. "I think you're forgetting something, though."

"Yes?

"You *don't* have to do it all yourself. Who ran the school while you were gone Friday and Saturday?"

"Preeti came in special on Friday to work, and Mr. Avi did Saturday on his own," Taemin said, brow furrowed. "And they had assistant instructors."

Marcus nodded. "You've got support. And *they've* got keys. You could stand to take a night off once in a while. And, okay, I won't pretend that I'm not hoping you'll spend that night off with *me*, but even if you just need to give yourself a mental health day, that's important too."

Taemin bit his lip. "You're right. I know you're right. I just… I haven't been in that mindset for so long."

"No time like the present, right?"

Taemin nodded, expression rueful. "But I probably still will go back to old habits at least once in a while. I need you to be patient with me. And tell me in ways that don't sound like I'm… like I'm not good enough."

Marcus swallowed. "I'm really sorry I came off that way." No wonder Taemin had been furious. "I'll do my best to be better."

Taemin smiled at him. "Thank you."

Chapter Thirteen

TAEMIN AND Marcus spent the rest of Sunday quietly. They went back to Taemin's place and he did some correspondence work—much of it letting people know about his injury and what he was able to do for the next few weeks—while Marcus made a few phone calls and looked over some paperwork of his own. They went to pick up some groceries (Marcus insisted on driving over walking over, and he was the one who pushed the cart), and they made lunch together. They watched a movie, spent some time reading their own things.

It was very domestic, and Taemin wanted so many more days like it. Just… quiet moments in between the rush where he had someone to be with. That he didn't need to do anything *but* have someone to be with.

Now they were back on the couch. It would probably be time to make dinner soon, but for right now they were curled up together, both on their phones, not needing to speak—just being with each other.

"What time do you have to be on set tomorrow?" Taemin asked. He himself had contacted all his early-morning sparrers to let them know he was cancelling classes for the week, just to give him some more time off the mat. He'd referee next week, and hopefully actually be back in the ring himself come July.

"Nine. Not too bad." Marcus waved his phone. "We're filming out in Detroit all day, though. I'm going to melt into a puddle."

Taemin chuckled. "Please don't. I think it'd be very difficult for me to kiss a puddle."

"Well, I mean, if you tried real hard…."

Taemin laughed and shifted just enough to kiss the corner of Marcus's mouth. Marcus caught his chin to kiss him again, a little more thoroughly. When they pulled away, Taemin smiled shyly up at Marcus, decision made.

"I'd like to see more of you," he said. "And… and I know that having me go to bed late and wake up early isn't a good way to do that."

"Really not," Marcus said, voice wry.

"So… so I was thinking…." Taemin took a breath. "It really would be easier if we started and ended in the same place, at least once in a while."

"I…." Marcus's eyes widened. "What?"

Taemin shrugged, trying for nonchalant. "If you wanted to spend a few nights here. I—I'd like it if you did. Just to spend some more time together. I know that we're still new, but… considering our schedules I just… wanted to offer."

"Are you kidding? Yes. Yes. I'd love to."

"All right," Taemin said warmly. "Why don't we figure out how that's going to work?"

"MORNING, BILLY," Marcus said, meeting him on set Monday. "How're things?"

"About the same as they were when we saw each other Saturday," Billy said. "Did you have a nice day off?"

Marcus beamed. "Yeah. Yeah, I did." And more to look forward to; he had an overnight bag already packed and waiting at his short-stay apartment. He'd be swinging by the dojang after classes that evening to keep Taemin company while he finished up for the night, and then they'd be driving separately over to Taemin's place, where Marcus would stay over. He'd get to go to sleep with him and wake up with him. He couldn't wait.

Billy squinted at him. "You're surprisingly chipper, compared to Saturday. I'm guessing things went well for him? Did he make it?"

"Oh, uh… actually no. He didn't."

"Oh." Billy seemed unsure of how to react. "I'm… sorry. But you're… not upset?"

"We talked," Marcus said. "And… and things are good. He's bummed about the loss and fuck, I'm bummed for him, but he's trying to use it as a chance to, like, reevaluate some of his schedule. And training routines."

"Oh," Billy said again. "That sounds promising."

"Yeah," Marcus enthused. They'd spent some more time talking over Taemin's schedule, and where and how he might be able to give himself some more rest. Even if not regularly, but on a possible week-to-week basis. "We're hoping it'll be a good thing."

"It's good that there's a 'we' again," Billy said after a moment. "You were moping pretty hard."

Marcus shrugged good-naturedly. Billy wasn't wrong. "I'm glad that there's a 'we' too."

"THAT *SUCKS*," Preeti said with feeling, when she came in and saw Taemin's leg for herself. "Oh my god, I'm so sorry. Did they disqualify the guy who did it?"

"They didn't need to," Taemin said. "He got a penalty for the hit, but since it was clearly not intentioned, he didn't get disqualified. I won the match regardless. The match after just exacerbated it."

"But you got *so close*," she moaned. "So close!"

"I know. It's okay." It was. He was trying to make it be. "We can't regret things that already happened. Regret doesn't change the past, just makes us dwell on it."

"Right! And you got the bye, didn't you?"

He nodded.

"Okay! Okay, so you can go back in four years. That's not so bad."

Taemin raised an eyebrow. "Four years is a fifth of your entire life."

"But! It'd only be a tenth of yours, by the time you were ready to go again. You could totally do it."

"Maybe," Taemin allowed. "I'd have to plan my training differently, though, if I were going to try to make it."

"Differently how?"

He sighed. "Actually take rest days for one. Real ones."

She blinked at him, wide-eyed. "Really?"

"Really," he said wryly. "I have been convinced that I might need to work a tiny bit harder on taking care of myself."

"Master Choi, that's great!" She looked so excited it was almost insulting.

Taemin rolled his eyes. "Don't let it be said that I never made my own self-improvement. Or that I couldn't admit my own mistakes."

"Can I be here when you tell Mr. Avi?" she asked, eyes shining.

Taemin sighed. "I suppose so."

THINGS SLIPPED into a pattern over the next few weeks. They both worked hard as usual, and sometimes would go for days at a time without actually seeing each other. But they texted and called in between spaces they were available. And Marcus usually spent at least one or two nights a week over at Taemin's. They fell into the habit of spacing those nights out a little to cut down on time they spent completely apart.

And though they often spent more time in than out, taking breaks from the world after hours spent dealing with it, it was time they both enjoyed, just getting to be in each other's company. They ended the night with dinner together—and they started making more use of Taemin's kitchen—or a movie if they had the time, but sometimes just sitting next to each other, or more often curled around each other, on the couch doing their own thing but with proximity.

There were nights, especially on Taemin's end, when all he was able to do was fall into bed. Marcus reveled in those days all the same, because he still got to be in bed *with* Taemin and wake up to him. That was enough. Even though he did, for the most part, prefer the nights where they both had the energy for more.

Taemin was still leaving the dojang around two or three on Saturdays, but it was with a break to eat. He did paperwork while he digested, then spent an hour on the mat instead of what had, in the last few months, become a usual two. He used the time after to run his errands and do chores so that he really *did* have nothing to do on Sunday but make it a lazy day of sleeping in, basic stretching—and nothing else, aside from a fifteen-minute warm-up. On Marcus's end, Saturdays were often a shorter filming day for him too. He finished up around six and usually swung by Taemin's once he was done. They'd gotten into the tradition of cooking together, prepping meals for the week, eating a quiet dinner in, sometimes watching a movie, then turning in for an earlier night.

If Marcus wasn't working on Sunday, they went out for dates. Taking trips to parks, walking around various downtowns, exploring new restaurants. It was idyllic and everything Marcus could have ever wanted….

And he got lazy.

"Bad news," Billy said one Monday morning. He'd insisted that he and Marcus meet for an early breakfast. Now they were tucked away in a corner of a buzzing Starbucks, and Billy was pulling out his tablet and showing Marcus some pictures.

Him and Taemin at Kensington. Sitting together—sitting *close* together, on one of the park benches. They were facing each other, Taemin telling some story from Saturday that had his hands in the air, while Marcus was laughing. Marcus's leg was hooked around Taemin's ankle. It was a good shot. Romantic. If it had been the result of *anything else*, it would have been something Marcus would maybe want to have in one of his own albums to treasure.

Now he was reading a headline of "Economi-watch Catches Our Hero In Action: Has Our Heartthrob Found His Leading Man?" with a sinking heart.

"Someone caught you in the park," Billy said, stating the obvious. "And it was enough for tabloids to run with it. And then they started putting it all together."

There were more photos. Some with just Marcus: on the phone, smiling wide, with the caption "Talking To His Love?" But others were of the both of them, leaving a restaurant, beaming at each other in the parking lot. One was of Marcus getting out of his car in front of Taemin's apartment building.

Furious, Marcus looked up to Billy. "What do we do?"

Billy glanced away. "Damage control. Release interviews. But there's one more thing you need to see."

Trepidation overtook him as Billy flipped to the last image. It was a close-up of Taemin's shirt. The ever familiar "Choi's Taekwondo Academy" logo was circled in red. "Ladies And Gents, We've Tracked Him Down!"

"Fuck," Marcus whispered, staring down at it. "When did this come out?"

"Just this morning," Billy said quickly. "So we've got a little time. When does he run classes, again?"

Marcus swallowed, shaking his head to clear it. "Mondays are his early-morning sparring class, but he didn't text me after it, so chances are that wasn't an issue. But he does his work with the homeschool co-op at one. That runs for an hour, and then regular classes start at four thirty."

Billy nodded, glancing at his watch. It was a little before eight. Marcus was slated to be on set at nine. "Okay. Okay, so I've got a little time. I'll make some calls. And you should too; talk to him, and then I will. The best thing to do to head this off is by you making it legit." Right. Getting rid of the speculation would help things die down at least a little.

"Okay. You release any statement in my name that you think will help. I officially sign off on it."

"Good. I'll try to convince him to cancel the co-op meeting, if just to give us some time to see what the reaction might be to this. If the paparazzi rush his school, then we need to be ready for that. We need to get *him* ready for that."

"Right. Yeah."

Billy looked at him. "Have you talked to him about this at all? About this sort of thing happening?"

Marcus frowned at the table. "Some. Back when we first started dating. And then nothing happened and I—I got comfortable."

"You're allowed to go out and have a good time," Billy said briskly. "You still should be, even with this coming out. And it *might* not blow up."

Marcus sneered. "Yeah. Like we both believe that."

"Talk to him. Let me know when you're done, and then I will. We'll get this sorted out. I promise."

Marcus could only hope.

AS WAS his routine, Taemin finished with his morning sparring class, then went home to take a shower, eat breakfast, and fit in a nap before he went about the rest of his morning to afternoon of training, paperwork, and getting ready for the co-op.

His phone rang just around eight forty-five, flashing Marcus's name. He was a little confused when he picked up. By now, Marcus should be on set, fifteen minutes early as he always was, and starting his day.

"Hello?"

"Taemin," Marcus said in a rush. "I need to talk to you. And then Billy needs to talk to you. Do you have a minute?"

"Sure," Taemin said, no less confused but now a little worried. "Is something wrong?"

He listened to Marcus explain what had happened with growing concern, if only because of how frantic Marcus sounded about the whole thing. "All right," he said when Marcus was finished. "Have Billy call me."

"Yeah, okay. Fuck, I am so, so sorry." It was about the fourth time he'd apologized in less than ten minutes.

"We'll figure it out," Taemin assured him. "Try not to think about it. You have work to do."

"Right. Yeah."

"I'll talk to you later, okay? It'll be all right."

A shaky breath. Taemin could picture Marcus raking a hand through his hair. "Yeah. Yeah, okay. I'll talk to you soon."

They hung up. Taemin's phone rang about thirty seconds later.

"Hi, Billy."

"We need to get together," Billy said briskly. "How soon can you meet me at the Dunkin' Donuts by your crossroads?"

"I can leave now, if you need me to."

"Good, great. I'm already on my way there."

"Okay, I'll meet you."

"Okay. I should be there in ten."

"All right."

"And Taemin?"

"Yes?"

"Be… be careful. Someone might be stationed at your apartment."

"You think they'd be dangerous?" Taemin asked, shocked.

"Shouldn't be, if it's just a photographer, but I just want you to be aware that someone might be watching."

"Okay," Taemin said. "Okay. I'll see you in a few minutes."

They hung up. Taemin took a second to stare at his phone in disbelief. Then he went to put on his shoes.

"SO WHAT'S going on?" Marcus asked Billy as soon as he had a moment to talk.

"He cancelled the co-op for the day," Billy said. "And he's prepping Preeti. Since they both usually get to Choi's at three to train together and stuff, he's letting her know what might happen. Aside from that, there's not a whole lot we can do until we see what does happen today, but at least he's warned. That's something."

"Yeah," Marcus muttered. "That's something."

Billy put a hand on his shoulder. "It'll be okay. You couldn't have gotten a more down-to-earth guy. He'll be able to handle it."

"I don't want him to have to," Marcus burst out. "And him being so down-to-earth might just make this even more overwhelming. He's not used to being in the spotlight. At least the other people I dated were already in the industry. They knew what to expect."

"And every paper I could get my hands on confirmed the rumors so it isn't a big, juicy surprise story that tabloids'll get to make money off speculation. You asked for your fans to respect your privacy, explained that things are new and that you don't want to scare him away—everyone loves a romance, and you've got a rush interview with *People* tomorrow afternoon. It's a start."

Marcus rubbed a hand over his face. "Yeah, okay. Thanks, Billy."

"That's what you pay me for."

PREETI CALLED Mr. Avi, who insisted on coming in even as Taemin protested. "You don't even work Monday nights," he said. "It's your day off."

"Yeah, and you could use the help, just in case. Don't worry, I already have a plan of action."

"I… okay?"

Mr. Avi nodded. "I think it'll help."

Mr. Avi's plan turned out to be him planting himself outside the door of the academy in his dobok and black belt and only letting in current students. Everyone else he essentially growled at, turning them away. "Master Choi isn't currently accepting new students," he told every one of them, many of them teenagers, though there were a few adults in the mix too. "And the academy is currently closed for private lessons. Sorry."

He did not, in fact, sound or act very sorry.

But it did mean that classes, for the most part, still went smoothly. The people who stuck around, pointing cameras and cell phones at the window, Mr. Avi approached and threatened to call the police on. That got most of them to take off.

One man called his bluff. Mr. Avi called the local police station and put his phone on speaker.

The man left.

A few hung around in the parking lot next door and tried to go over to students and families as they were entering and leaving the building, but it was almost amazing how they all refused to engage. His school had his back. And that was—just such a wonderful feeling.

When the last class had been dismissed, Taemin checked his phone to see a message from Marcus, asking him to call when classes were over.

"Taemin! Hey."

"Hi."

"How-how did things go?"

Taemin told him.

"Oh my god," Marcus said when Taemin was finished, sounding so relieved. "Oh my god, that's great. Okay. Okay, that's manageable."

"Mr. Lin volunteered to do the same thing tomorrow," Taemin said. Mr. Lin was a student of about a year and a half, and he would be testing for black belt at the next sixth-month mark. He was also six foot three and built like an absolute brick wall. Even Taemin had some trouble doing takedown throws on him.

"Your students are actually the best," Marcus enthused. "And if they keep it up for like a week or two, a lot of the interest will die down, except for maybe some of the junkier rags. We'll still probably get followed for pictures, though. I… I hope that's okay."

"I can't say I love the idea of people intruding on our life like that," Taemin said honestly. "But it's part of your life, and I want to be a part of your life too. I'll live with it."

"I wish you didn't have to," Marcus said wistfully.

"Me too." Taemin shrugged, not that Marcus could see it. "But we have to deal with the reality. So we will."

A sigh. "God, you're amazing. I—how are you taking this so well?"

"I love you," Taemin said simply. Because it *was* that simple. "It's worth it."

There was a sharp intake of breath. Followed by a shaky, almost awe-filled "I love you too."

MARCUS WAS shocked—but ridiculously pleased—that not much changed. He and Taemin still had their busy schedules, and they still tried to make time to see each other as often as they could. Sometimes Marcus had twelve-hour days on set; sometimes Taemin had an exhibition or a tournament or a seminar on the weekends. They were still followed. Billy kept a running tab on all the media. Taemin had been approached for a few interviews, all of which he politely but firmly turned down. They made it work.

Then, on a Monday in the middle of August, just after seven fifteen, Marcus got a text message.

Please don't come by the Academy tonight. Meet me at my apartment instead?

Sure, Marcus sent back, a little confused. *Everything okay?*

Just fine. I just need to get some surprise last-minute work done. I'm cancelling classes for the day, even, to do it.

Oh, okay. Well hey, if you don't have classes, can I come by a little earlier tonight then? I should be done by seven.

Please do! I'll see you then :)

Awesome.

It was a little weird for Taemin to cancel things so last minute, in part because when he did, not only did he send out an email and make a Facebook post about it, but he took the time to call each and every family. It could take *hours*. Marcus wondered what had come up.

When he checked his phone during a break in his own filming, it had blown up with messages from Preeti.

Marcus, oh my god, Marcus.

Did Master Choi tell you what happened?

Can you believe it?

It's DISGUSTING I can't actually believe it.

Except I had to, because it happened.

I'm calling everyone on the roster to let them know what happened. Master Choi obviously doesn't want me to give details but I'm GIVING THEM.

Normally it takes like TWELVE FREAKING WEEKS from estimate to install, but luckily Ms. Marissa's husband is a contractor and they're doing like a rush job, especially considering the circumstances. Measurements today so manufacturing can start tomorrow and hopefully it'll only take like six-eight weeks, but since the dojang is basically made of windows, that's just an estimate.

We're closing for the entire week, just to make sure everything is cleaned up. Broken glass on mats with people in bare feet? Not a good idea.

Running classes starting next Monday though. We're putting plastic and stuff over the windows as soon as we finish calling everyone.

Let me know when you get this. I need to have fucking words with your fan club.

Marcus stared at the messages. He hadn't heard anything from Taemin except for the text that morning. Marcus had just assumed he'd be ridiculously busy calling his students. And apparently he *was*—he and Preeti both were.

Broken glass? "Considering the circumstances?" His *fan club*?

What the fuck had happened?

He called Taemin and it rang six times before Taemin picked up. "Marcus! Hello. How's filming going?"

"What happened?" Marcus asked.

"What happened to what?"

"Did something happen at the academy?"

"Oh! It's nothing to worry about."

Marcus frowned. "Preeti said something happened to the windows."

"Oh, that. It's nothing, really. Just an accident. Needed to do some surprise repairs."

"An… accident," Marcus said slowly.

"Made a slight mess," Taemin said. "But again, nothing to worry about. I'll see you tonight still?"

"Um, yeah. Sure."

"Okay, great. Have a good day!"

"You too."

They hung up. Marcus immediately dialed Preeti. "Hey," she said, sounding furious. "I know, right? I just—*fuck*."

Preeti didn't swear. "What happened," Marcus demanded.

A sharp pause. "He didn't tell you?"

"Tell me *what*?"

"Some fucking bastard threw bricks at our windows."

Marcus went cold. "What?"

"Yeah. With notes on them and everything."

"What—what did they say?"

"'You're not good enough for him,'" Preeti growled.

The fury was immediate and all-consuming. "*What*?" he hissed.

"You heard me."

"Fuck, I—*Fuck*."

"Yeah."

"He—he didn't tell me. He didn't want me to know."

"Probably didn't want to make you think it was your fault," Preeti said. "You know how he is."

It was his fault. It was absolutely his fault. "I need to go," he said. "I have some people to talk to."

"You better."

They hung up. Marcus ran to Billy, on the phone in a corner. Marcus grabbed his arm. "Hang up," he said. "I need to talk to you yesterday."

Billy took one look at him and hung up without saying goodbye. "What's going on?"

"I need you to get to Choi's and do whatever you can to figure out what fucking nutcase shattered their windows."

"What?" Billy said with horror.

Marcus's phone buzzed. He pulled it out of his pocket to see another message form Preeti. *Image attached.*

He opened it, then shoved his phone at Billy, unable to breathe. All but one of the windows was just shards of jagged glass, the intact one cracked beyond recognition. He closed his eyes and saw *you're not good enough for him* flash behind his eyelids.

Billy stared at Marcus's phone, face a storm cloud. "I have to make some phone calls," he gritted out.

TAEMIN GOT to his apartment feeling exhausted, even if it was hours before he normally got home on a Monday. He had swept up the glass. He and Preeti had called all his families. Ms. Marissa, who was part of his early-morning sparring class, had immediately volunteered her husband's services, which Taemin felt incredibly fortunate about. He had, upon her instruction, gotten tape and plastic to cover the windows for the time being.

Preeti had gotten rid of the bricks, because it made Taemin feel sick to touch them.

But now he was home, and he could try to put it out of his mind until tomorrow, when the contractors came for measurements. Until he saw his school again, covered in plastic because someone was—was hateful.

Try not to think about it. He'd see Marcus soon. That would be nice. Even if he couldn't tell him what happened, just his presence would be a comfort.

And he *couldn't* tell him what had happened. Marcus had already been so unhappy with even the idea of people finding out about their relationship. About them bothering Taemin. With this….

He hoped Marcus never found out.

He ended up flopping down on his couch and closing his eyes. Tried to meditate, even if all he could see was the academy covered in broken glass.

The buzzer in his building rang out loud and startling. Taemin was grateful for the distraction. He let Marcus in and was suddenly walked backward into his foyer, Marcus kicking the door closed behind him before he enveloped Taemin in a hug. "I'm so glad you're all right. I'm so sorry. I'm so sorry." He pulled back to cup Taemin's face in his hands. "Why didn't you tell me?"

Taemin averted his eyes.

"Taemin, come on, please."

"I didn't want you to worry," Taemin said quietly. "You already worry about so much when it comes to me. My health, our privacy, the school. You take it all on and blame yourself. I didn't want to do that to you. It's not your fault."

Marcus scowled. "Of course it's my fault. None of this would have happened if it hadn't been for me. And this—this was an *attack*."

And this was exactly why Taemin hadn't wanted Marcus to know. He knew he'd internalize it. "The fault is with those who did it," Taemin said. "It's no more your fault than it is mine."

Marcus's eyes widened. "You—don't say that—you're the only innocent party here!"

Taemin stepped back and then took Marcus's hand, leading him to the couch. "I love my school," he said, voice still soft. "I love my students, and I love what my parents and I have been able to build. And I love you. Windows can be replaced."

Marcus stared at their linked hands. "It's not fair," he said at last. "It's not fair this happened to you. Or to me. But it's also—" He cut himself off, frowning hard.

"Yes?"

"Why didn't you *tell* me? I had to find out from Preeti. And—what, you just—you were going to try to keep me from going over to the school for weeks? Or give me the runaround about why you were suddenly missing all your building's windows?"

"I—"

"I'm not stupid. And I get that—that you didn't want me to worry, but—but I'm supposed to. I'm *supposed* to. I love you. I'm going to worry about you. In big things and little things. And… and you need to let me."

It was a fair point. Taemin worried about Marcus too. Obviously he did. And he'd only been trying to protect him, but… he could admit that he'd been short-sighted. "I hadn't even thought about what I'd say tomorrow," he admitted. "Just that I didn't want you to know today."

"It's… yeah," Marcus said after a moment. "Yeah, I—you had a lot on your mind. I get it. But just… don't try to keep me away like this. Please? I—I really have…." His fingers tightened around Taemin's own before they relaxed. "I've really, really enjoyed being a part of your life these last few months. Of being able to love you. And I don't want to be kept away from the bad stuff. That's important to share too."

"Okay," Taemin said. "I mean, you're right. Of course you're right. I'd want to know about things that made you unhappy. I'd want to know when you were sick or scared. I should give you the same courtesy."

This close to Marcus, he could see him swallow. "Thank you."

They drifted into silence.

"Did you eat dinner yet?" Taemin asked, several minutes later.

Marcus looked up, startled. Then he smiled. "Wait, you're asking me if *I* ate?"

"Well," Taemin said loftily, "I've been a lot better." He had, after all, had plenty of practice in the last few months. "So, have you?"

Marcus shook his head. "I haven't, to be honest. I came here as soon as I was done on set. It was, uh, it was hard for me to really think about doing anything else."

"Hm. Forgetting to eat because you're concentrating on other things. I can't *imagine* what that's like."

Marcus huffed a laugh. "Okay, okay. Would you like to order in?"

Taemin shook his head. "I have plenty of food in my fridge."

"Oh, hey, do you have any of the baked ziti from yesterday left?"

Taemin gave him an amused look. "No, Marcus, I finished almost an entire baking tray of pasta today by myself."

Marcus almost looked like himself again when he said, "That sounds good to me, if it does to you."

Dinner was still quiet, subdued, as the events of the day processed. Marcus had been too distracted on set to really pay attention to anything past saying and doing what he was supposed to when he was supposed to, so he didn't have a whole lot to tell Taemin.

"All my downtime was working with Billy about what I want to release about what happened."

"Release?"

"Yeah. That shit is not okay. I want to make sure my fans are fucking clear on that note."

"So what are you going to do?"

Marcus sighed. "Not enough. Mostly just try to take over as much social media as I can. Paint things in as negative light as I can make it. Just… try to get that across. Is there anything you want me to say?"

"Me?"

"Yeah, you know. Anything in particular you'd like me to mention."

Taemin opened his mouth to say no, then hesitated. "I think it's a good idea to make sure people understand that this didn't just harm *me*. I have almost five hundred students who train at Choi's every week. They're from all walks of life and backgrounds and circumstances. Having the school closed suddenly doesn't only mean that they lose the chance to be there, but they also have lost the safety that my school provided. I can sweep up glass and pay for windows. I can't give back a child's sense of safety."

Marcus bit his lip. "Yeah," he said at last. "That's… that's a point I didn't even think about. I'll make sure to call attention to that."

They spent the rest of dinner bouncing ideas off each other on what and how Marcus could say what he wanted to. Billy had managed to arrange for a radio interview spot for the next morning. An early one, which would give the rest of the radio stations plenty of capability to grab sound bites of their own.

As for the reality of the situation, Taemin admitted there wasn't a high chance of actually catching who had done it. "We don't have security cameras on the property. There'd be no real way to trace the perpetrator." That was obviously hard for Marcus to take.

He did also beg Taemin to let him go in on the contractor job to get the windows replaced. "I know you said that it's not my fault. I won't argue with you about how I feel. But I want to help. I *need* to be able to help. I have money. Please?"

"Why don't we talk about it more later," Taemin suggested. "Ms. Marissa's husband just took measurements today, so I won't have the estimate until tomorrow anyway. Once I have that, we can discuss that. Okay?"

"You promise that you're not going to just try to put me off?"

"I promise," Taemin said gently. "Now come on. It's been a high-stress day. Why don't we make it an early night?"

Chapter Fourteen

HELLO LADIES and Gents, readers of all types! We know you've been dying to find out what's been going on with Hollywood's biggest heartthrob, Marcus Economidis, in both his professional life AND his personal one! We already all know what's out there: he's working on a hot new movie, Volkor Rising. *Big cast, big characters, larger-than-life sci-fi plot. With a scorching romance of course!*

Speaking of scorching romances, the other hot new thing in Marcus's life is his new boyfriend! After several less than savory sources splashed a pleasant evening across tabloid pages, Marcus has come forward to confirm that yes, the rumors were true. Officially spoken for! He released a few statements (one of which was published in yours truly) about wanting their privacy respected but went pretty quiet on the details. This was especially interesting considering that Marcus's man is very much an out-of-the-spotlight kind of guy. He's got nothing to do with Hollywood and doesn't work for the industry at all. Instead he's the owner and Master Instructor of Choi's Taekwondo Academy in Michigan. AND get this—that so happens to be in the area where Marcus grew up.

That's right readers, we are happy to report a good ol' fashioned homegrown romance has bloomed. But don't take it from us, take it from the man himself! We're happy to welcome Marcus into our midst today!

Popsugar: Hi Marcus! Good to see you. Thanks for taking the time to come and talk with us today.

Marcus: Thanks. And sure. I think there's a lot of good stuff to talk about.

Popsugar: No kidding! And we have plenty of questions about how the new movie is coming, but first, we can't help ourselves—are we allowed to ask you about your new romance?

Marcus: Sure. But you know… it's actually not that new anymore.

Popsugar: It feels like it, since we never got much info. Care to share? When did you two meet?

Marcus: We met right when I got in to begin filming, back at the start of May.

Popsugar: And it's September now! That's a good chunk of time.

Marcus: I know. I can't believe it. I don't know what I did to make him think I was worth keeping around, but I'm doing my best to keep it up.

Popsugar: Oh stop, you know you're a catch.

Marcus: Thanks. I'll tell him you think so.

Popsugar: So? When did those sparks start to fly?

Marcus: Pretty much since I laid eyes on him. I basically followed him around for a week. Managed to work up the nerve to ask him out and… and he said he'd give me a chance.

Popsugar: If you could see his face right now, readers. He's absolutely lovestruck.

Marcus: I'll freely admit that.

Popsugar: Have you had any issue with dating someone not in the Hollywood scene?

Marcus: Actually, yeah. Yeah, I have.

Popsugar: Oh no, what's been going on?

Marcus: Well, we talked about a lot of what to expect. Particularly the lack of privacy. That's really important, especially since Taemin runs his own business. If people go bother him to try to take pap shots and stuff, that really interferes with his job. And his job is mostly about kids. So that really, really isn't okay.

Popsugar: You look like you have more that you want to say.

Marcus: Yeah, I do. I'm sure you heard what happened to his school. And for readers who don't know, a supposed fan of mine smashed the windows in Taemin's building.

Popsugar: It was awful. We're so sorry.

Marcus: Yeah. Yeah, it was... not a good time. The building still isn't fixed either. It'll still be another six weeks before the windows are supposed to come in. We do know they're in process though, at least.

Popsugar: That's good news.

Marcus: Yeah. But on that note, I do want to say something to my fans and your readers?

Popsugar: Of course, go ahead.

Marcus: Taemin is one of the hardest working, most special people I know. He has dedicated his life to helping others. He has a scholarship program at Choi's, he volunteers, and he works with homeschool kids. And that's on top of running a school designed to boost self-confidence and build kids up. Whoever it was that tried to hurt him tried to hurt someone truly good. And on top of that, they hurt all the students Taemin had to turn away while the school was being repaired, all the students who showed up to a place they loved to find it damaged, all the students Taemin wasn't able to make his usual time for because he was dealing with hatred and jealousy. I like to think I can forgive a lot, you know? I'd never forgive that.

Popsugar: Totally, totally understandable.

Marcus: I think so too. And I know it brought the mood down a little, but it's something I've been needing to say. In a way I hope it gets heard.

Popsugar: Of course! We get it. He's special to you. You want to protect that.

Marcus: You have no idea. Though in terms of protection, I think he's got me beat in the "literal" camp.

Popsugar: That sounds like a story!

Marcus: Not a long one, but a funny one.

Popsugar: Please, go on.

Marcus: So as you guys know, I do most of my own stunts and fights, right?

Popsugar: We do, and we're VERY impressed.

Marcus: Haha, thanks, good to know. I'm proud of myself too and what I can do, but for Taemin it's a way of life and skill that I'll never be able to touch. But, you know, I'm bold. I wanted to show off. So I offer to spar him. Build it up too; say I'm going to give him a real workout… maybe flirting. Maybe.

Popsugar: And??

*Marcus: *laugh* He wiped the actual floor with me. A normal round is supposed to last two minutes. I think he tapped me out in points at thirty seconds. It was fantastic. I was in total awe. Still am. He's amazing.*

Popsugar: We heard a little whisper about him being an Olympic hopeful?

Marcus: Oh god, yeah. Not this year unfortunately. And that's not my story to tell so I won't go into details, but he's got a shot in another four years. I'll be rooting for him either way.

Popsugar: So will we!

Marcus: And I could go on about how much I'm crazy about him for ages, but I don't think we have enough time for ALL of that.

Popsugar: That's fair. In that case, can we talk a little bit about Volkor Rising? You're almost done with filming it, aren't you?

Marcus: Yeah, we're slated to wrap up in October.

Popsugar: That's only a month away!

Marcus: I know. We've been working really hard to make sure we finish within the originally estimated time frame.

Popsugar: Well, we believe in you!

Marcus: Thanks. I'll be sure to pass that along to the team.

"PREETI," TAEMIN said, exasperated, "I already told you that you don't have to come by. We're not running classes."

"I know we're not running classes. That's because you're finally getting the windows in. I want to see the new windows!"

"They'll look the same as the old windows, except that they won't be broken," he said dryly.

"Master Choi," Preeti said evenly. "I'm coming by today once I'm done with school. You can't stop me."

"I won't even be at the academy by then. The contractors should be finished installing everything by five."

"I have my own key."

"Oh fine, if you want to see them that badly—"

"Thank you."

"You know, they'll be there tomorrow too. When you're actually supposed to come in. They won't be going anywhere. That's rather the point."

"Then I'll see them tonight and I'll see you tomorrow. And okay, I got to my building, gotta go. Have a good day!"

"You too," he said before she hung up.

He shook his head fondly as he put his phone back in his pocket. Eight weeks after the incident at Choi's and today they were finally going to be able to take down the boards and plastic. He doubted anyone was looking forward to it as much as he was, but Preeti could probably give him a run for his money.

Marcus too. He'd wanted to come in for it, paying no mind to the fact that it was in the middle of the day in the middle of the week. Taemin had quickly nipped that thought in the bud, but he had promised to text him pictures of the progress. It was little after ten now, and the contractors were supposed to come at ten thirty. He'd been told that it would take around half an hour per window to deal with the detailing and cleanup, maybe a little longer just because each one was so massive. He'd decided to err on the cautious side and factor in about an hour per window, just in case. Even with that, they *were* supposed to be done well before five. And thus well before Preeti got out of her Wednesday classes and Marcus got out of filming.

According to Marcus, they were solidly in the home stretch of filming. He didn't have a clear idea of when London decided things would be over, but they were shooting a lot of smaller scenes that didn't need the same type of time and energy, even if the days were getting longer and longer. Marcus was spending almost every night over at Taemin's now, if only because sometimes that was the only time they saw each other.

It was so nice, though, to see him even for that little bit. Just being able to sit quietly with him, sleep with him…. Taemin treasured every moment.

And he'd really miss them.

Marcus was, after all, going to be done with filming soon.

They hadn't talked about it much. In passing, more than anywhere else. A few back-and-forth jokes about Marcus bringing Taemin with him to Hollywood—which was, of course, ridiculous, if only for the reason that Taemin could never leave Choi's—or Taemin offering that Marcus just stay with him.

It'd been said lightly. In teasing, in passing. But it'd been said. And Taemin was starting to think about it more seriously, now that the weather was turning cooler. In the last month, Marcus had essentially moved in anyway; all he'd really brought with him to his short-stay apartment were his clothes and some accessories, so those just… all eventually ended up at Taemin's. They weren't always around at the same times, but they didn't need to be. And sometimes one or the both of them weren't up to talking, and that was all right too.

He simply so much enjoyed having Marcus around.

But Marcus had an entire life back in California. It was where his parents lived, it was where his friends all were, and it was where his main place of business was. Taemin felt selfish even bringing it up because he didn't want to ask for something that Marcus might have to make himself refuse.

At the same time, however, he wasn't about to deny his feelings. He loved Marcus. He wanted him in his life in whatever way he was able to have him. It was a big step asking him to move in—officially move in—instead of going back to California. Marcus always could say no, and Taemin would be the first to assure him that he respected that decision.

But first he needed to make the offer.

"CUT! AND that's a wrap!"

The entire cast and crew burst into applause. Hailey jumped at Marcus for a hug, and he swung her around before setting her down again. "We did it!" she cried. "We're done!"

He grinned at her. "Yup. Great job."

"I am going to eat an entire thing of ice cream," she enthused.

"Yeah? What flavor?"

"Chocolate chip."

"Good choice," he said wisely before turning to smile at Leo, who'd come barreling at him for a hug himself. "Hey!"

Leo grabbed him up tight. "We did it! Man, we did it!"

Marcus laughed and hugged back, exchanged hugs and celebratory congratulations with basically everyone on set. There was a lot of talking and laughing and eager conversations starting up about when and where to host the after party.

"I can't believe it's over," Roger said from where he'd ended up at Marcus's elbow. "This was such an amazing project."

"And one of the longer ones you've ever worked on, right?"

"Oh yeah. This is over double what my last role was. I can't wait to go back home."

Back home. Right. "Missing Anita?"

"Of course. We talk every night and we've been FaceTiming and Skyping, but there's nothing like actually being *with* the person you love, you know?"

"Yeah," Marcus said with feeling. "I know."

"Good job," Billy said, coming up to him, expression proud. He held out Marcus's phone. "Want to tell the world?"

Marcus took it. "I've got the go-ahead?" Billy nodded. "Awesome. Roger, you want to be in the shot?"

"Sure."

Marcus slung an arm across Roger's shoulders and took a selfie of them both grinning at the camera. A couple of hashtags later and it was trending on Twitter and Instagram. The next thing he used his phone for was a much more private party. *Filming's officially done!* he sent to Taemin.

He got a reply back almost instantly, which was startling up until he remembered that Taemin had cancelled that night's classes to ensure there were no complications with the window installation. *That's wonderful! Two things to celebrate today :)*

Yeah! The windows look great, by the way.

I think so too. Would you like to do something to celebrate? Or are you going out with everyone?

That was a damn good question. Normally Marcus would be all for going out with everyone right now, especially since Taemin usually had evening classes at the same time. But he didn't today. They would both have a full evening. And tomorrow was Thursday, so not even an early morning for Taemin. *Could I come over? Maybe do our own little celebration? I could pick up dinner stuff.*

That sounds wonderful. Come over whenever you want. I'll be home.

Right, Marcus thought again. Home.

He'd been putting off bringing it up because he hadn't wanted to push or sound like he was trying to get a commitment out of Taemin, but he—he *had* been living over at his apartment more often than not, especially in the last month. And he hadn't enjoyed going "home" like that in years. He wanted to keep doing it. Or at least have the chance to do so.

He'd never ask Taemin if he could move in, but Marcus couldn't help but maybe look into some real estate around the area. Close to Choi's, in a nice neighborhood. Nothing huge, but a nicely sized house that would be good for two busy, active people.

Maybe… maybe more than two people, eventually. Though that was another conversation altogether.

Right now, Marcus just knew he loved his life and he loved Taemin, and he wanted more of the latter in the former. He worked in LA, but he also had money; he could afford to fly where he needed to be. His friends were mostly in the Hollywood scene, but they all traveled everywhere all the time. He was just as likely to see Leo again next week for lunch or in three months in New Zealand working on a new movie. Billy… was brilliant. If nothing else, he could work remote.

Marcus might have been mulling this over in his head for a while now.

TAEMIN KISSED Marcus hello and then stepped back to let him into his apartment. "Congratulations." he said again, smiling up at him. "How does it feel?"

"Not real yet," Marcus admitted. "Not until I meet with Billy tomorrow and we talk about what's next."

"Already planning, hm?"

Marcus stooped down to kiss him again. "You know it."

"So what sorts of things will you be talking with Billy about tomorrow?" Taemin asked curiously after they'd both sat down at the table and served themselves. "Surely you don't have something planned *right* away. Do you?"

Marcus shook his head. "Not in so many words. But uh… I do have some things to talk to him about in regards to our working relationship. Though that depends on something I wanted to talk to you about tonight, actually."

Taemin nodded. "I'm all ears."

"How… how would you feel about me staying in the area? For, uh, for a little more long-term."

Taemin stared at him. "As in moving here? To Michigan?"

"Yeah. I—I've maybe been looking at properties. Houses. Obviously no pressure, but I… I really want to be closer to you. I'd be up for doing the long-distance thing of course, but—"

"What about California? Your work?"

Marcus shrugged. "The world is pretty flat when it comes to the film industry. People fly from all over for auditions and to work on movies and stuff. I don't mind being one of those people. We'd honestly probably end up doing the long-distance thing anyway, at least some of the time, as I got new projects to work on. I'd just… I'd just really like to have you to come home to."

"Me too," Taemin said. "I mean, I've been thinking about it. I've wanted to broach the topic with you, but I wasn't sure how to do it."

Marcus took a breath. "Yeah?"

Taemin nodded. "Of course. I love you. I love having you in my life. And I'd love it if you stayed in the area. I, um, I wanted to offer my apartment."

Marcus's eyes went wide. "You mean it?"

"You've essentially been living here a month already. We fit well in each other's space. I know it's on the minimalist side, though, and if you wanted your own place, especially as we navigated what comes next—"

"I love your apartment," Marcus said. "And being in it. I just couldn't ask that you let me stay."

Taemin smiled. "You're not asking, I'm offering. For you to move in with me."

"Then yes," Marcus said fervently. "Absolutely, yes."

"I LOOK ridiculous," Taemin grumbled from their hotel's en suite living room. "I haven't worn a suit in years."

"A dobok is basically a suit," Marcus said absentmindedly as he did his tie in the mirror.

"Those are not even remotely similar to the same thing."

Marcus laughed and smoothed down his tie before ducking into the living room to see Taemin fully dressed in the dark green suit they'd decided on. It took Marcus's breath away.

"What?" Taemin said, looking down at himself. "I knew it. I knew I looked silly—"

"You look gorgeous," Marcus said, stepping closer until he could take Taemin's hand, press a kiss to his knuckles. "I'm the luckiest man in the world."

"Second luckiest," Taemin murmured, before pulling him down for a more thorough kiss.

They ended up having to check themselves over in the mirrors again to make sure they weren't too rumpled. Then they left their hotel room and made their way to the waiting limo.

Taemin reached for Marcus's hand again once they were inside. "I'm nervous. I've never even been to an opening night at the movies, much less a film premiere."

"I know it'll seem overwhelming, but it's really not so bad. It'll be loud, but I'll be with you. People will stop us for pictures and we'll smile. We might be asked questions and we'll answer them. If you're really uncomfortable, just let me know and I'll make sure we keep walking until we're done."

"Okay. Okay, I can do that."

"Just pretend you're on a mat instead of on a carpet." Marcus smiled. "It's all about presence. And you certainly have plenty of that."

Taemin rolled his eyes. "I'm not about to shout at your fans in Korean."

Marcus laughed. "Maybe just give them your disappointed look. You know, the one that makes your students wish you were giving them push-ups to do."

"Somehow I don't think that will be very effective against a large crowd of your screaming fans."

"At least they pretty much love you now," Marcus said, squeezing Taemin's hand. "Half my interviews are about me not being good enough for *you*. Especially after the Twitter thread about you and Kids Kicking Cancer that went viral a couple months ago."

"Yes," Taemin said blandly. "Because that's what matters to me most. Social media."

"I love you," Marcus said, full of affection.

Taemin turned to peck him on the cheek. "I love you too."

They arrived at the venue and their driver stopped the car. "Ready?" Marcus asked.

"Ready."

Marcus opened the door. The onslaught of noise was sharp and sudden but nothing he wasn't used to. And he was excited beyond measure to be sharing this part of himself with the love of his life. He stood, then turned and held out a hand for Taemin, who took it.

Showtime.

AIDAN WAYNE lives with altogether too many houseplants on the seventh floor of an apartment building, and though the building has an elevator, Aidan refuses to acknowledge its existence. They've been in constant motion since before they were born (pity Aidan's mom)—and being born didn't change anything. When not moving Aidan is usually writing, so things tend to balance out. They usually stick with contemporary romance (both adult and YA), but some soft sci-fi/fantasy has been known to sneak in as well, and they primarily write character-driven stories with happy endings. Because, dammit, queer people deserve happy endings too.

Social media:
Twitter: @aidanwayne
Facebook: www.facebook.com/AidanWayneWrites
Website: aidanwayne.com

Also from Dreamspinner Press

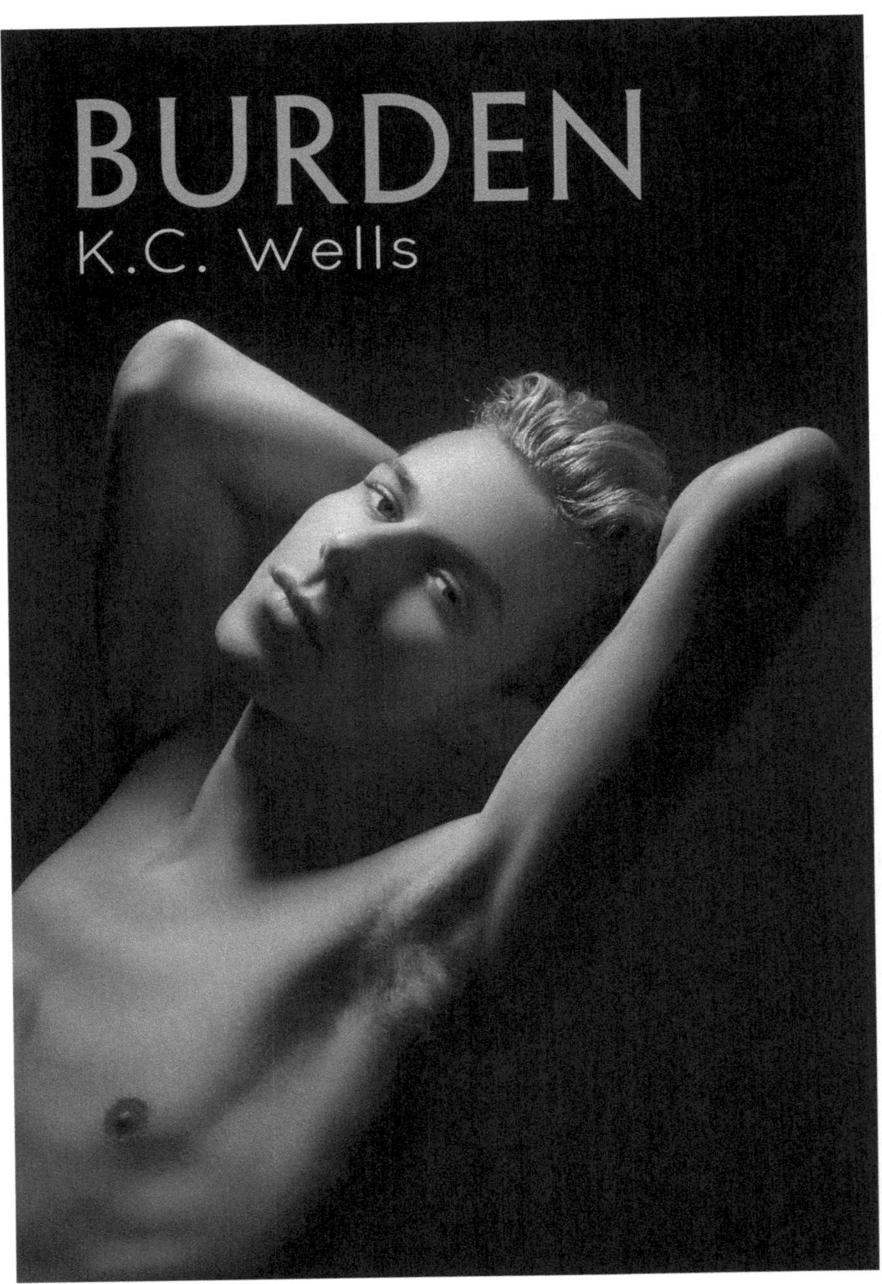

www.dreamspinnerpress.com

Also from Dreamspinner Press

www.dreamspinnerpress.com

Also from Dreamspinner Press

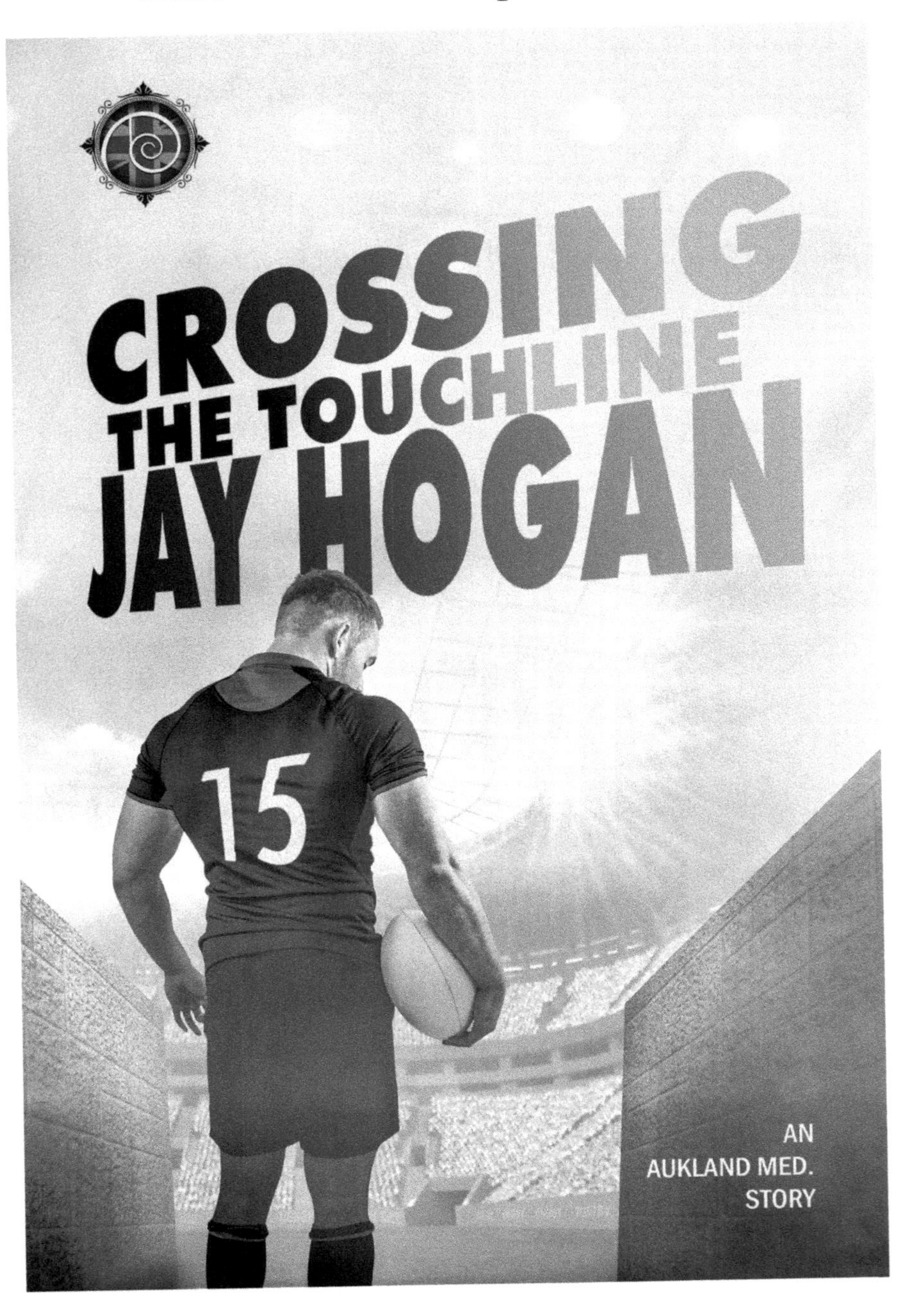

Also from Dreamspinner Press

www.dreamspinnerpress.com